THE ALTRUISM EFFECT

a novel

KRISTIN HELLING

THE ALTRUISM EFFECT
by Kristin Helling

Printed in the United States of America
First Printing, 2017
ISBN 978-1-946921-99-4
Adrenaline
An imprint of Wordwraith Books, LLC

705-B SE Melody Lane #149
Lee's Summit, MO 64063

e-mail wordwraiths@gmail.com
website www.wordwraiths.com
Twitter @Wordwraiths

Edited by Ellen Campbell
Proofread by Reece Hanzon
Cover Design by Rob Allen @n23art
Format Design by Kevin G. Summers
Kristin's email author@kristinhelling.com
Kristin's website kristinhelling.com

The Library of Congress Cataloging-in-Publication Data
is available upon request.

For my husband, Austin for his immeasurable support.

For all those involved in Sterling and Stone's Apprentice program (Including but not limited to Ric Beard, who held my wordcount accountable).
For my business partners, J. R. Frontera and Rod A. Galindo of the Wordwraiths.
For Nick Brown, for his extensive beta notes.
For my Mom and Dad, who have always protected me from the likes of the monsters in this story.

Without the above, this series would not be possible.

TABLE OF CONTENTS

ONE

The stench of chemicals clung to the hairs inside her nostrils as she reached up and clutched her hand around her neck. She attempted to swallow and lubricate her dry, scratchy throat.

I've been drugged. Her eyes fluttered open and scanned the damp concrete her cheek was smashed against. As she lifted her head, a splitting pain erupted at her temples. She groggily looked around to realize she was in some kind of holding cell.

How the hell did I get here?

As she strained to recall her last memory before she woke, a bright light illuminated the cell and forced her arms up over her face. "Hello?" she asked the light.

Two bodies emerged on either side of her and hoisted her up to her feet.

She winced as her limp ankles dragged across the floor. "What's happening? Why am I here?" She hardly recognized her own voice, rough and scratchy.

The two strong figures brought her into a room that was floor to ceiling in white tiles. She strained her eyes against the starkness of the room, and noticed the only break in the white was a mirror along one wall. The pressure from the men on either side of her stopped, and she crumpled to the floor.

The heavy door slammed behind them.

Using what strength she had left, Raine Walsh pushed against the tile floor and stabilized herself on all fours before grounding each foot. She stood shakily and turned to the mirror.

Tears quivered in her eyes as she stared back at the stranger in the reflection. She reached up and touched her tangled, straggly hair. The chestnut strands were caked with a black sticky substance that emerged at her hairline. She leaned closer to the mirror and shoved her bangs up. Blood. The crusted crimson was stark against her skin. She stared into the broken blood vessels in the whites of her eyes, and turned her head to peer deeper. A sick feeling in her stomach told her that someone was staring back. She pushed off the mirrored wall.

The door chinked open and two men entered the room. She hadn't gotten a good look at the two that brought her here, she didn't know if they were the same men.

Raine scanned their tan uniforms and duty belts, fully equipped with guns, batons, and cuffs. As far as she saw, they were guards. Cops. "Help me please, I don't know how I got here and I'm injur—"

"You have the right to remain silent."

She pursed her lips and furrowed her brow at the guard. *They're here to help me, right?*

"—Anything you say, can and will be used against you in a court of law. You have the right to an attorney. If you cannot afford an attorney, one will be provided for you. Do you understand the rights I have just read to you?"

Raine crossed her arms over her chest. "My name is Raine Walsh. I'm a licensed psychol—"

"Do. You. Understand the rights I have just read to you?"

She couldn't look into his eyes because he wore large, reflective sunglasses. Both of the officers were wearing dark shades.

She croaked, "Clearly this is some sort of mistake."

The lead guard nodded over to the other, who reached for the baton on his belt.

"Yes! I understand, I understand."

"We weren't able to perform intake for you because you were brought in unconscious. Now that you are... coherent, will you comply so we don't have to restrain you?"

A sense of panic tightened around her body. She focused on her breathing, the only thing she could control. What else could she do? *Comply.* She nodded her head.

"Good. Now strip."

She didn't quite understand at first. She looked down at herself, then back up at the two guards. The lead guard stepped towards her. The other stood back by the door. He appeared aloof as he stared into the corner of the room, away from her, with purpose.

"Take off your clothes and put them on the floor to the left." His voice did not falter.

Raine felt the panic constricting her throat. "Can I have. . . female officer?" Her voice was almost inaudible, just above a whisper.

"The second you came through those doors, you forfeited your right to privacy. There are no female officers in this facility. Strip."

She saw no other option but the baton. Raine reached down and shakily slipped her fingers into the waistband of her black yoga pants. She shimmied them down her thighs and yanked them off her ankles, inside out. She wasn't about to give them a show, and even though she worked through a splitting headache, her balance was on point.

Yoga pants . . . She pressured her brain into trying to remember what she was doing before she was knocked unconscious. It was as if a slice of time had been removed from her memory. These pants might have indicated that she was going to or from a class, but not in her case. When Raine wasn't wearing the business casual attire that she wore to her office as a clinical psychologist, she was often found wearing exercise clothes. She could have been knocked unconscious and brought here at any time.

Next came her top. An oversized, magenta tee shirt that she peeled up and over her head, then tossed on the floor with the pants. Her eyes were drawn down to some deep purple bruises on her ribs. She ran her fingers lightly over the tender area as she looked sideways at the mirror on the wall. The chill in the white tiled room pricked the skin on her arms, raising goose bumps.

"Faster."

She winced at the sound of the lead guard's voice, and reached up between her breasts. Her racer-back bra was clipped in the front. With her fingers trembling, it was a challenge to grip the clasp. She unhooked the bra and let it fall back off her arms. She leaned forward and inched off her underwear, moving it over on the floor with her foot.

She crossed her arms over her chest and stood in the stark room, avoiding the gaze of the men in front of her. As she heard a clink of metal, she lifted her eyes and saw the lead guard reach for a hose clipped on the wall next to the door, one she hadn't noticed before.

He clutched a gear and twisted it to the left. A hissing sound filled the space. He turned back to her. "Spread your arms and legs."

"Why is this necessary?" she whimpered.

"Do it!"

She closed her eyes and turned her head to the side, spreading out her arms like a bird and parting her feet. As she moved her right foot out, it seemed to sink into a slight dip in the tiled floor. She cracked open her eyelids to see a drain at her feet. She was beyond the knots in her stomach and the aching of her body at this moment, but something of a raw energy emerged through her limbs. She was humiliated. Exposed.

She recalled studying inmate behavior in prisons during her time at Stanford University when she was fulfilling her doctoral psychology degree. When an inmate was admitted, they'd literally and figuratively strip them of their identity.

The next step is always water. The cleanse. Just as the thought crossed her mind, the stream ripped into her body. Even though the guard was at some distance, the water pressure was just too much for her 110-pound frame. The pain was consuming and her knees buckled. She held her arms out as best she could, the freezing cold water felt like it was skinning her. She dropped her head and caught a glimpse of the muddy water. First, it shot out of the hose clear, but became tinted with her blood before it swirled down the drain.

"Turn!"

She heard his terrible voice over the water and spun around, exposing her back to the jet. Hair clung to her forehead and cheeks in soppy strands. He finally finished, and hung the hose back on the clip. Without waiting for approval, she fell forward onto her knees on the cold, wet, tile. The door opened behind her, but she didn't dare look.

"Your uniform." The voice was softer this time. She assumed it was the voice of the hands-off guard that stood by the door. The door slammed with an echo that bounced off the corners of the room.

Raine turned and crawled to the crumpled pile of fabric. The grout in the tile pinched her knees, but she focused on the terrycloth fabric underneath the uniform. She grabbed the navy blue towel, one that had probably been used by many before her, and wrapped her body. She dabbed at her pink, tender skin to dry herself.

As she wrapped her hair in the towel and squeezed the water from it, she glanced back up at the mirror. She'd almost forgotten it was there. That *they* were there, whoever was surely watching. She reached for the uniform, which was essentially a hospital gown like smock: a sheet with holes for her arms and head, that tied up the back.

The longer she stared into the mirror, the more questions arose in her mind. And with every question, frustration played across her face.

Where am I?

Why can't I remember what got me here?

Who can I trust if not the police?

Despite her exhaustion, she had the intense urge to run up to the mirror and bang her fists on it. But before she could do anything, the door opened and two different guards came in. The others must have been the intake guards, and these were the transport guards. They flanked her and half dragged her through the door.

She struggled to keep up with their pace. Her eyes darted all around as she tried to soak up any understanding of her environment.

They dragged her down a long, dark hallway, lit only by a few caged sconces with Edison bulbs inside them. Not long after, they arrived at a pair of large, metal doors. The guard to her left reached into his pocket and retrieved a ring of jangling keys. He shoved the key inside the slot, pushed one side open, and they guided her into the room.

When Raine turned the corner, a sinking feeling in her stomach took the place of curiosity.

Before her was a massive warehouse. Her eyes scanned up concrete walls to the tall ceiling with its exposed metal rafters. Though what gripped her with terror were the rows upon rows of cages. As they forced her down one of the rows, her eyes absorbed the sight of the concrete cubbyholes, each stuffed with a cage the size of a large dog kennel.

And inside each cage, a person.

She started to struggle wildly and the guards tightened their grip on her arms.

One of the guards wrapped her in his beefy, muscled arms and nearly squeezed the breath out of her. He grunted, and his shoulders swayed back and forth as she fought.

The guard in front grabbed her chin and looked into her eyes. His eyes were a sickly, olive green. He reached into his back pocket and pulled out a syringe.

Her eyes widened. She tried to turn her face from him, though when she saw him bite off the cap of the syringe and toss it aside, she let her body go limp. There was no use fighting. They were stronger, and she was outnumbered. She would have to continue to comply, and try to think of a plan as she went along.

The man behind her loosened his grip, and she gasped with relief. She doubled over and clutched at her aching chest.

The guard behind her pressed the palm of his hand into her spine and pushed forward.

As she stumbled forward she caught a glimpse of a lethargic man crouching inside his cell. The cages weren't even big enough to stand in. She was shoved forward to an empty kennel.

"Why?" she screamed, as she searched the caged faces for answers. Silence. It seemed as though the other people were immune to noise.

The man behind forced her onto her knees.

She dropped her head down as tears welled in her eyes. She crawled across the hard ground and into the cage. There was just enough room for her to turn around as the man slammed the door shut behind her, rattling the entire structure.

He locked it, and then turned to leave.

"Why am I here?" she screamed again as they walked away. She raised her feet in front of her and kicked at the door of the kennel. As she rattled the door, what the guard said next stunned her into silence.

"Second degree homicide." He raised his arms. "Welcome—to the place for murderers."

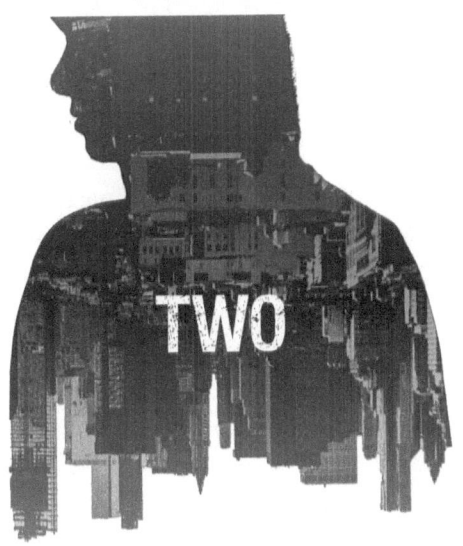

TWO

Nothing made sense.

Second degree murder? I could never... She slumped back in the cage and pulled her knees to her chest. Her bare bottom pressed against the cold concrete and she wrapped the excess of the gown tightly around her legs.

"What is this place?" she shouted again, though the guards were long gone. None of the other caged people seemed interested in speaking with her.

The moment she had entered this warehouse and saw the cages, she'd understood this was not a state facility, if it was even legal at all. Her memory was still foggy. Exhaustion played the colors of her emotions inside her closed eyelids.

Confusion.

Frustration.

Paranoia.

"It's no use."

Her eyes fluttered open again as she heard the voice from the cage next to her. The tone was raspy and husky, as if the wind had been kicked out of him as well.

Raine crawled forward and smashed her face against the grate of her own cage, trying to see who spoke from the cell next to her. She wasn't able to see who it was directly, since there were barriers in between each cage.

She felt a sense of urgency at the sound of his voice. She wanted to talk to somebody coherent. *Maybe he can give me some answers!*

As she looked down the line of cages across from hers, each person inside was like a zombie, lethargic or lying down.

She thought carefully before she spoke. "How come it's no use?" she asked quietly as she continued to press her face against the metal door.

"They won't answer you. They won't give you any information."

"Are they okay? The others over there?" She slipped her hand through the bars in the front of the cage, to point at the people across from them.

"Just as good as me and you. Saving their energy for when it matters, I suppose."

Saving their energy…

"How long have you been here?" she asked.

"I've lost track." He sighed and kept his voice low.

"Do you know why we're here? Surely. I didn't— I'm not a murderer." *Is that pushing it?*

A silence loomed between them, and she'd thought for sure she blew it.

"I've been trying to figure that out since the day I got here," he finally said.

Raine stretched her legs out to the back of the cage. She stayed quiet a moment, as questions ran through her mind. "Why the hospital gown?" she asked and looked down at the garment.

"To strip you of your individuality. Make you vulnerable." His voice was drained, even more so than before. "What's your name?"

She thought a moment. Could she trust him? What use would he have for her name? *The gown is used to strip us of our individuality, but they can't take our names away.* "I'm Raine," she answered, her eyes welling up unexpectedly at the sound of her own name on her lips.

"Well, nice to meet you Raine. My name is Arie."

She saw movement out of her peripheral vision. She turned her head to see fingers that reached out of his cage, and curled around to the front of hers.

The corner of her mouth twitched up into a small smile. She put her fingers through the cool metal as well, just managing to touch the tips of his fingers for a makeshift handshake.

Even though she'd just gotten here, she felt as though it'd been an eternity since she'd been in her normal life routine.

She felt a connection with him.

It comforted her.

And the silence between them told her that it comforted him as well.

THREE

Meditation hadn't always come naturally for her. It was a practice she'd had to work at. Though in this moment, behind the cold metal bars of her cage, she felt grateful for the art. She closed her eyes and began her breathing routine. In for four seconds as her belly expanded up to the rib cage, then out for four more as she caved into her spine. Her mind became a blank slate as the sights, sounds, and emotions of the prison faded around her.

Two weeks ago

A smooth woody fusion with effervescent notes of bergamot and iris wafted across her nose as Raine pulled back the door to her office. She held it open for the woman inside to pass into the lilac-walled waiting room. A receptionist sat at a desk made from a kitchen table across from a river rock water feature.

"Julie, just keep working at what we talked about, okay? You've got all the right tools. You just need to use them. And you have my number if you have any questions. We had a great session today."

The curly haired woman in her forties reached out to shake hands with her. "Thank you so much, Dr. Walsh."

Raine smiled warmly at her and squeezed her hand gently. "It's my pleasure, as always. Sylvie can set up a time for your next visit." She motioned at the receptionist. After one last smile, she turned and headed back towards her office door.

She noticed the door next to her office was cracked open. She peered inside at her fully equipped yoga studio, which she used for therapeutic yoga and meditation. The light from the window reflected sunbeams onto the ancient original hardwood floors—one of the many benefits of restoring an old home into a therapist's office. She reached forward and pulled the door closed.

She looked over her shoulder to see both doors on the opposite side of the waiting room closed as well. Her eyes fell upon the plaques that bore the names of the two colleagues who went in on the co-op office with her. Doors shut meant they needed to check with Sylvie before entering, to make sure they weren't with a client, the common name they used to replace the term "patient." Though doors shut this late in the day could also indicate that they had gone home.

As her client Julie headed out, Raine moved into her office and secured the door. As she stepped to the couch she curled her toes in the soft, shaggy carpet under her bare feet. Throw pillows were askew on the sofa where she helped so many clients reach clarity in their lives, and she reorganized each one back to its original spot. A glass of burning incense sat on the coffee table. She loved to use scents in therapy. Sandalwood was a great relaxer for those with anxiety, something she treated on a daily basis.

Just as she moved over to her armchair to gather the papers on the end table next to it, the door creaked open. Without turning around she spoke, "Sylvie, did you get a schedule worked out for Mrs. Handson?" She collected her papers into a folder on the chair. The door shut again.

"Damn, you look good in those pants."

Raine leaped up and spun around. "Marcus . . . what are you still doing here?" She crossed her arms, her lips twitched into a small smile.

"I had a session run late," he answered, glancing at his watch. "How was your day?" He moved towards her.

"Oh you know... I've made some progress with—"

Marcus slid his arm around her hips.

She stifled a small laugh, "—a few clients. Man, you're handsome." She pushed her hips into him and grabbed the back of his neck. She stretched up on tiptoes and placed her mouth on his, giving a gentle kiss as she reached back and ran her hand along the waves of his buzzed, black hair. Marcus had full lips that she could kiss over and over again, but the awareness of their location came back to her as she dropped down on her feet and turned to grab the folder.

"Last night was fun." He reached up and unbuttoned the top two buttons of his shirt, and then pulled at his necktie to loosen that as well.

She smiled and nodded. "Yeah... we should probably be more careful here at work, though. We need to keep things professional."

"Professional?" He smiled at her with his straight, white teeth.

Raine laughed. "What if Troy finds out about us? And even if he did, I'm not entirely sure we're more than casual?" she teased.

"Naw, we're just having fun. Professional fun."

She laughed. "I'm serious!"

"Oh come on, Raine… " Marcus sat in her armchair. "Troy has the same status in this co-op that we do. Plus, he's been hanging around us since University. I'm sure he already suspects something is going on, and he hasn't done anything about it."

"Sure he has."

"What are you talking about?"

"C'mon, Marcus! You haven't seen it?" She walked over to her filing cabinet and pulled open the second drawer, filing away the folder from her last session. She closed the drawer and reached into her pocket for a small set of keys attached to a lotus flower keychain and locked the cabinet.

"I can't even walk from the water feature to my office without getting the side eye from him." She turned around and leaned against the cabinet.

"You must be just imagining that."

She threw her hands in the air. "Imagining it? Right. Yup. That's what it is." She walked over to her closet, grabbed her shoes and slipped them on her feet, then grabbed her bag off the hook inside.

"Oh, come on, now you're angry?"

"Of course I am! You know how many times Troy has crossed the line? He's even made Sylvie uncomfortable, watching her sitting while he walks in and out, in and out of his office all day!"

There was a knock at the door. A pang flipped her stomach and she gave Marcus a look before calling out, "Yes?"

The door cracked open and Sylvie said, "I'm going to head out now. You two okay? Need me to take any cases home?"

Raine relaxed her shoulders. "Naw, thanks so much Sylvie, I'm going to stay a little late and finish up some paperwork. We'll see you tomorrow."

"Bye Raine. Try and get some sleep tonight."

"Bye Sylvie!" Raine and Marcus called out in unison.

"Bye to you too, Marcus... " she trailed off, and shut the door behind her.

Raine collapsed on the couch. "You think she heard us?" She looked up at him, her words dripping with guilt.

"She didn't," he whispered. He moved from the armchair to sit next to her. "You worry too much. Hey, look. I'll keep an eye on Troy, okay? If he makes you feel uncomfortable—"

"He does."

Marcus let out a long sigh. "I'll take care of it."

"I hate asking you to butt in. Most things I can handle on my own. But that boy doesn't know when no means no. He's disrespectful. And not just to me." She liked that Marcus was there for her. Her whole family was back in Ohio. After getting her graduate degree at Stanford, she decided to stay in the San Francisco Bay area to start her life. Being so far away from her family, it was nice to feel security in the person in front of her.

"I know you can handle it." He pushed back a strand of hair that had fallen in front of her face.

She warmed as he tucked it behind her ear.

"I love this… little line on the side of your mouth when you smile. It's not quite a dimple, it's—I don't know. It's beautiful. You're beautiful."

She couldn't help but smile as she reached up and touched his cheek. His brown complexion was flawless. She pulled close to kiss him once more. "All right, Prince Charming, I've got to get in the other room and start some restorative yoga." She twisted his wrist towards her to look at the time on his watch.

"Do you ever stop working?" he asked.

She laughed. "Self-care, right? You have to take care of yourself if you're going to take care of other people. It's been a long day. You should understand, with all your mending of relationships with adolescents on probation and their families."

He nodded. "Yeah. It's exhausting." He reached up and rubbed at his eye. "And rewarding… Can I get you some dinner, maybe get take out and bring it back here?"

"Not tonight. I brought some granola with me. But after I do yoga and finish up my paperwork, I should get home to Viona. She's been cooped up in the house all day and I'll need to take her out to the dog park."

"How about we plan a date night some other time, then?"

She paused a moment, reading his amber eyes. "I'd like that," she whispered.

He smiled and stood up from the couch. "Text me when you get home tonight, okay? I don't like you being here so late on your own."

"I will." She returned the smile, and then opened the door to her office for him to leave. As he went across and locked his own office, she glanced over at Troy's door. He must have already taken off for the day. Lately he'd been heading out early, which was the reason she decided to stay for yoga in the first place.

Troy hadn't always been a womanizer. Sure, he appeared to be a ladies man at Stanford, but he seemed to respect her at least. She'd heard stories from some of the other girls in her classes, but she'd always just minded her own business. It wasn't until Marcus suggested they went in on a co-operative office with him, that she hesitated before agreeing to work with him.

As she watched Marcus leave, locking the glass door behind him, she was beginning to think that it was going to be hard to not want something more than a casual relationship with him.

She moved from her office to the studio next door. One of her stipulations for moving into the office with the boys was that she had her own studio in addition to an office. It was an important part of her lifestyle and practice. She moved into the room and turned binaural beats on the stereo. The repetitive, relaxing rhythm came through the speakers.

She rolled her yoga mat on the floor and sat. She stretched her legs out in front of her and took a deep breath, expanding her belly and rib cage, before releasing everything out that wasn't serving her.

It was Marcus who had convinced her to join the co-op. He argued that Troy came from a family of high status, and he'd have the credibility in the industry to give them a good start. Since he came from money, he was able to buy the house. He could pay for it outright and they wouldn't need to rent the space.

She brought her attention back to the euphoria of the music, the scent of the room, and the mindfulness in her soul. These things fueled her day to day in this mentally exhausting profession that she couldn't live without.

As she turned onto her stomach and pushed up into a cobra stretch, she heard a loud bang coming from reception. She glanced toward the door.

"What the... " She turned over and hurried to the stereo, paused it, and listened.

Next came a series of bangs on the glass that rattled the front door. Her heart raced, pounding against the inside of her chest cavity as she hurried to the door and threw it open.

There, in the spray of light from the porch, was a man in his late fifties, banging his fists on the front door. When he saw Raine, he fell to his knees, continued to rap on the door, and called out.

Darkness surrounded the porch light and the man that knelt under it. How long had it been since Sylvie and Marcus left? Had she lost track of that much time?

She felt conflicted as she watched the panicked man. He wasn't her patient. She didn't recognize him. It was late. And she was alone at the office. This situation broke all safety protocol of the office, and quite frankly, all of the rules she lived by. But clearly the man was in distress. He needed help.

Raine had a curse. She inherited the human emotion of empathy. She became a psychologist to help those in need. Against all common sense, she rushed to the door and unlocked it, then placed her hand on the knob. *Shit, where's my phone?* As she opened the glass door, the man fell in at her feet, sobbing.

"Hey, what's going on? Hey... hey now." She patted his shoulder. She tried to see if she recognized the balding man. She still didn't.

"The office is closed now. Who are you trying to reach?"

"You... you are... " He inhaled audibly through his sobs.

She knelt down on the floor by his side. "Breathe deeply. In two three four, out two three-"

"You are Dr. Walsh?" he gasped, grabbing her arm.

She flinched. *Keep calm.* She tried to wriggle out of his grip, but he was strong. She swallowed and pasted on a professional face. "Sir, if you'd like to make an appointment, I can see you during office hours. If you aren't feeling well now, I can call an ambulance." *Where the hell is my phone?*

"I don't want an appointment. I came here to tell you—" He cried again, almost hysterical, breathing sharply and loudly—all signs of a panic attack.

Take control... She reached under his arm and hoisted him up, then guided him over to a couch in the waiting room. "Look. Look here," she instructed him, holding her index finger in front of his face. "Look at my fingernail. It's painted. What color is it painted?"

The man avoided her gaze.

"My fingernail."

"It's painted gray."

"Good. What shade in the gray family?"

His breathing smoothed as he focused on the one, small thing. "It's a charcoal color."

"Good. Now tell me who you are. Why are you looking for Dr. Walsh?"

"My son… my son is Aaron Brittle," he croaked as he looked up from her fingernail.

Raine racked her brain. *Aaron Brittle. Brittle. Brittle.* "He's one of my clients."

"Was."

The air in the room grew thin. "What do you—no… "

"You were supposed to help him! Your job was to cure him!"

"What happened?" Her voice was just above a whisper. "I'll be right back, I need to get my—" She stood. *Phone. I need backup.* She couldn't handle this on her own. When she turned toward her office, the man grabbed her arm again.

"You're hurting me." Her voice was throaty.

"He hung himself."

Raine reached her hand up to cover her mouth. "But he was doing so well—we were… making progress." Her eyes flicked back and forth.

"You murdered my son, Dr. Walsh. He came to you for help and now he's gone. He's gone!"

FOUR

The overwhelming guilt ripped her from her meditation as the memory of that night in her office surged through her mind. Raine weaved her fingers through her hair, and closed her fists around it. She remained sitting with her back to the door of the cage, the metal bars pressing into her back. She'd rather stare at the back of the cage than at the others in their boxes across from her.

How can I remember the details of that night weeks ago, but I can't remember yesterday? She racked her brain until her head throbbed. The obvious solution was to blame it on the drugs she'd been given, but her professional training told her that it was because of trauma. Sometimes the mind will choose to block out information that is painful or devastating to remember, or deal with, until it's ready. Part of her job was to tap into those moments with patients and help them deal with and overcome them, so they could move on with their lives. She was fully and consciously aware of this, but couldn't fathom conducting this strategy on herself without help from another therapist. Right now, she needed to devote her energy to the burning questions that kept her from falling asleep like the rest of the murderers.

Why am I here?

How did I get here?

How can I escape?

It was that first question that drilled into her head. *Why.* She pulled her hands back from her hair and observed them, front and back. The mauve nail polish was already nearly chipped off. She'd changed her polish from charcoal to mauve since the day she met Aaron Brittle's father.

Maybe it was my fault, she thought, as she remembered the sessions she'd had with Aaron. She should have been able to help him pull through. She should have received updates about his wedding and the success of his career, not of his death and date of when the funeral would take place. Even though he took his own life, she felt responsible. He knew that he could call her in times of emergency. But if his emotions were pushed to the limit, strong enough that he felt the only way out was to end it, then she failed. She did murder him.

I am responsible. She let out a short, exasperated sigh.

As she closed her eyes to the darkness, an alarm resonated through the warehouse. Raine reached up and covered her ears against the miserable high-pitched tone with underlying mechanical banging noises. She turned to look both ways up and down the row. People in the other cages were stirring. She felt as though the alarm was imbedding itself into her skull, as if it would never go away.

"Arie!" she cried out, and pressed her face against the bars. "Arie, what's happening? What does that mean?" Her throat constricted. When Arie didn't respond right away, she was worried he was gone for good.

Just when the isolation set in her bones once more, she saw his fingers stick out by the edge of their cages.

"Shush, it'll be all right. It'll pass."

"How can you be so calm? Does this happen often?" she yelled over the sound of the clanging.

"Often? I don't know. It's sporadic. I think they do it to keep us awake. Sleep deprive us. Torture."

Raine moved closer to the corner of her cage to hear his voice better.

"Though some just sleep through the alarm now too. It'll be something new, next."

"How many... people are here?" she asked, trying to remember what she saw as she walked through the warehouse.

"I don't know. Can't be more than twenty? Some of the cages are empty. But that's just a guess. We don't interact very often."

The alarm diminished, though the tail end of the noise echoed off the ceiling rafters to the other side of the warehouse. Rigid stillness replaced it.

"Arie are you... are you a murderer?"

He slowly retracted his fingers. A silence hung between them, and Raine felt it despite the horrifying clanging of the alarm still ringing in her ears.

"Are you?" he asked back.

She slumped down in her cage. "I feel responsible for the loss of a life. Yes." She couldn't tell whether or not he heard her soft reply. He didn't respond, which could mean that he did or didn't hear her, either way.

The door to the warehouse creaked open and four men wearing bulletproof vests marched in and opened several cages, dragging the people to their feet. It happened faster than she had time to think.

She thought about calling out to them, asking why she was here and why they were taking only certain people, but fear froze her. She remembered Arie saying there was no use trying to get them to answer you. She watched as one by one, people were taken from their cages. She scooted into the back of her cage and hid. She thought they were getting ready to leave, but then the sounds drew closer.

They weren't coming for her. She saw Arie jerked into the view in front of her cage by the hand of a guard.

A chill jolted up her spine and wrapped around her neck as she caught a glimpse of his face. His ash brown hair framed his forehead, but his features were calm, though he had dark circles under his eyes. As his arm was twisted and he was yanked down to the concrete, he turned and looked directly into her cage.

"Arie!" she shouted and scrambled to the front of her cage as quick as her jelly legs would allow. She wanted to help him. Frustration gripped her and her fingers wrapped around the bars as she yanked on them and shouted, "Take me too!"

Arie's eyelashes fluttered and she thought she saw him shake his head slightly at her. He wasn't resisting, he couldn't resist. She remembered the syringe, the kind of leverage these people had. He couldn't have been more than seventeen or eighteen years old.

She watched them take him. And she wondered if it would be the only time she'd ever see him.

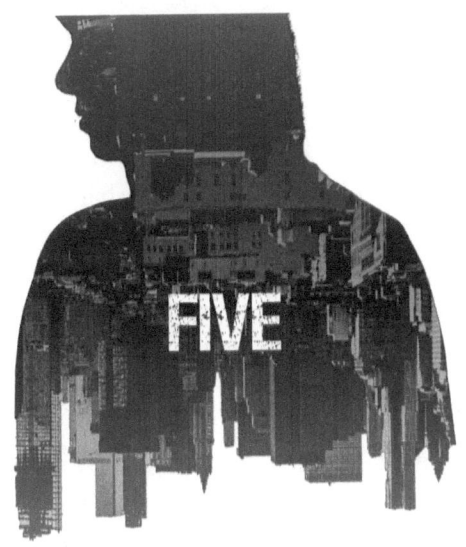

FIVE

The longer Arie was gone from the warehouse, the more time she had to think about what horrible things could be happening to him. Her thoughts drifted from the cage to waking up in the intake room. Before she was even admitted, stripped, and forced into this gown, she'd woken up sore. Every muscle in her body had ached and throbbed.

She moved her wrists back and forth, and stretched her legs out in front of her. Clearly nothing was broken, but she definitely had aches and bruises from an event she couldn't remember. She pulled her arm through the hole and into the gown, fingering her ribcage where she had seen the purple bruising. Nothing bothered her more than the time that was gone from her memory. The moments that led her to where she was now.

There was one other time in her life that she remembered blacking out, apart from this. Raine had been at a bar with her friends, dancing the night away to celebrate a promotion. Just remembering her friends, with the colored strobe lights across their faces and the taste of cranberries with vodka on her tongue, brought her out of the confines of the cage.

Though the blackout from the bar incident had been different. She'd woken up in the bathroom of one of her girlfriends' apartment in downtown San Francisco. She'd gulped orange juice and aspirin as her friend recounted all the things she had done that night that she found hilarious, things Raine knew she would never do sober.

After she'd seen the evidence of the night before in the toilet she was draped over, she'd made a vow to never allow herself to get to that point again. She'd hated the idea of not having control over her own body or mind. It had become almost an obsession for her, an extreme to the point where she practiced methods of bringing her consciousness to a heightened state, through meditation or hypnosis.

She brought her attention back to the stillness of the warehouse. Her eyelids were heavy and her lashes closed over her eyes like a curtain. *It's my job to counsel families and relationships that are in turmoil—to be their guide into the light at the end of the tunnel, not to be in turmoil myself.*

The clunky metal door to the warehouse screeched open.

A sobbing girl with dirty blond hair emerged from behind the door with one of the muscle men behind her, guiding her by her ponytail. He yanked her hair to the left and forced her into one of the cages. Just behind her was another guard, this time dragging Arie in his wake.

Horrified, Raine covered her mouth. Arie's head hung, and he looked small and weak, dragged behind the large man. As he was about to be placed back into his cage next to Raine's, he lashed out and put up a fight.

The guard brought his fist down hard on Arie's face. Arie swung back.

Raine pushed herself to the back of her cage again. Every muscle in her body tensed up.

During the commotion, the other guard used his keys to open her cage.

Her legs shook uncontrollably. *He has no idea he's putting Arie in my cage!*

The guard shoved Arie into her cage and slammed the door. Arie had clawed the man's face pretty badly, and it looked as though he was having difficulty seeing.

The heavy lock clicked and the guard rushed out of the warehouse, cursing as he went.

Raine held onto her knees in the fetal position, just inches away from Arie. "Holy shit, are you all right?" she whispered, and reached her hand out to him.

He looked up at her. He had a deep purple and blue bruise on his cheekbone, circling above to his brow. "I... I," He collapsed.

She reached out and shifted his body the best she could, so his head was in her lap.

He was out cold.

She was drifting. Raine snapped her head back up, and rubbed at her eyes. She looked around, realizing she was still in the cage with Arie. The warehouse was nearly pitch black, with a few bare bulbs along the wall by the door. She calculated it must be nighttime, but she couldn't be sure. Her internal clock was definitely telling her it was time for her body to rest, but she felt as though she didn't want to. It was as if by closing her eyes, she might miss out on some major clue that would answer all of her questions.

In the dim light, Raine traced the lines on Arie's face with her fingers. He was attractive, in a humble sort of way. He had a long nose, with high cheekbones. When she reached his eye, she lifted her fingers, remembering the skin was torn open and swollen.

Must have been from when he was whacked in the face by the guard, she thought as her stomach squirmed at the thought of the pain he must have felt. He was younger than her, probably around the age of her little sister, she imagined. When she first saw him, she thought maybe seventeen or eighteen, but now that he lay in her lap, she thought him to be a little older. He must have been in his early twenties, probably around twenty-two. His limbs were long and lanky, and underneath the gown that he wore, she imagined she'd be able to see the definition of his ribcage and hipbones.

Arie moaned, and turned his body to get up.

"Shh." Raine soothed him and stroked his hair.

He shuddered at her touch and opened his eyes wide. "How did I... ?" It was as if it were painful for him to talk.

She leaned into him. "Shh, it's okay. I don't think they know they put you in here with me. The guard was in such a hurry to get rid of you and leave, that he just picked the first cage." She spoke at just above a whisper. "You put up a pretty good fight."

He shuffled awkwardly in her lap and put his hands on the floor to push himself upright. "Yeah but now it'll be worse... for me. Next time." He groaned. "Night guard is a douche."

She laughed under her breath. "Is the one you decked the douche?"

"He takes the power trip a little too seriously, so I stuck it to him."

Raine moved closer to the front of the cage to give him more room in the little space they had. She looked out to see if anybody was watching them from the other cages. She leaned forward and whispered to him, "Why not just... comply? That was my plan."

"Well, that may work for you."

She smoothed the gown over her legs. "What happened to you when they took you?" she asked.

Arie sighed.

"I'm sorry," she said, "you don't have to talk about it if you don't want to."

"They just brought me into a small room and played mind tricks."

"Mind tricks?"

"Well yeah. Make me repeat numbers over and over. Strap me to a chair and hit me when I don't listen. Do push-ups. Any kind of stuff they can think of to break me down."

"I'm sorry. That's awful."

"They're trying to disorient us." He shuffled next to her.

"I'm scared."

"Well, turn that fear into a solution. I have a plan to escape," he whispered.

His warm breath fogged her ear and she straightened as she caught up with his words. "You do? How?" she asked.

"Megan. She'll help us. She has connections."

"Megan? Who's that?" she whispered.

"She's like me and you. Well, kind of. She was brought here, only she's sort of like a favorite for the guards. She gets special privileges and things."

"How do you know you can trust her?" she asked as she listened intently.

"She's one of us, Raine. She used to sleep in one of these cages herself. She understands what it feels like to be locked up and not know why or what their purpose is. Now the authorities here trust her."

"But how do you know she's not just trying to convince you she's trustworthy to figure out what your escape is, so she can tell the guards?"

"She hates it here. She's... I think she's given up a part of herself to survive in here. We've gotten pretty close since I've been here. I just know... I trust her." Arie said.

Raine felt a twinge of jealousy. It surprised her. She looked away from him and furrowed her brow.

He reached for her hand. He picked it up and put his other hand on top.

She felt the comfort of his touch, but a part of her was nervous so close to him. She thought of her damp and clammy hands, something he didn't seem to care about at all.

Jealousy is an emotion that never gives, it only takes, she thought. Her irrational jealousy over Arie's connection with Megan, a girl who'd had to *give herself* to survive, was replaced by guilt. She didn't even know this guy so close to her. He'd been the first being in this environment that comforted her, and she had latched on in desperation.

What about Marcus back home? *Marcus*... Where was he? Did he know she had been brought here? Was he even looking for her? The thoughts seemed to bog her down in confusion even more so than before. "How come she's given in? Why has she given a part of herself to survive?"

Arie sniffled in the low light. "She complied." He dropped her hand and turned his head away from her.

The word sent chills across her. She slumped as she looked down into her lap. "What are we supposed to do?"

"Well, Meg has seen more of the prison than a lot of us. She says if you follow the hallway all the way down to the end, you run into a set of stairs that go down. She thinks the only way out is down."

"Have you ever been up?"

"Yeah. The guards call it "yard time," time for us to stretch our legs and get some air. It's been a while since I've been up there."

"Up there?"

"Yeah, I think the yard is on the roof of where we are now. Every time I've been up there, it's been foggy as all hell. Meg's had more yard time than any of us. But I tell you, there's no way we'd get away by going up."

He seemed so clear, so sure of it, that she didn't question him. He'd been here longer than her. He knew things she didn't.

"So our job is to find a way out of these locked cages. How do you propose we do that?" she asked.

"Well, I think—" He coughed, hacking up blood into his hand. He turned away from her again.

"Hey... they got you pretty bad?"

"A few—" he coughed again, "kicks in the internal organs oughta do it." He spoke between coughs. "It's gross. I'm sorry." He wiped his hand on his gown.

She furrowed her brow once more and raged inside that she couldn't help him. *Can't believe there are people in this world that would do this!*

"I think we just need to wait for another guard to come get us, and then we attack them," he said.

She thought about it a moment. "What if they come prepared?"

"There will be two of us this time, not just me or you. We can take a guard, the two of us."

She hesitated a moment. "Well then, it's crazy, but it sounds like we have the beginning of a plan." Raine breathed deeply.

"But before we can try to take out a guard, we need to get our rest. So try your hardest to get some sleep. I know you haven't slept since you got here."

She peered into the shadow over his face as he spoke to her, with just the light from down the row of cages shining dimly across them. His eyes wore a look of concern. This young man, who had just been beaten to a pulp, still cared about her well being. He had the virtue of a protector inside him. It was comforting to have a comrade in this environment.

She turned her head to look at him. "How would you know if I hadn't slept yet, unless you haven't been sleeping either?"

She hadn't slept well since she awoke in the intake room, and she'd already lost track of the time spent inside her cage.

Arie moved towards her.

She wasn't entirely sure what he was doing. She sat still as he adjusted himself next to her, shoulder to shoulder.

He reached over and gently placed his hand on the side of her head and brought it toward him.

She laid her head on his shoulder. In the dark of the cage, they sat together, the motion of their breathing moving in sync. Her eyes fluttered closed.

She drifted.

SIX

Raine woke, and snapped her head up. She oriented herself in the cage once more. *I don't think I'll ever get used to this,* she thought, as she looked out of the cage at the others across from them. Part of her felt like the others weren't even human. She never talked to them. They never talked to her. From the moment she was thrown into her own cage, she saw them as murderers. And she did not classify herself as one of them.

But she wasn't alone. Arie was there too. Was he like the others? No. He couldn't be. Arie was like her, thrown in here by mistake. Treated like dogs. Worse than dogs.

She looked over at him and saw his eyes were wide open. He raised his index finger to his lips to shush her.

The door to the warehouse opened, and pounding footsteps echoed off the walls.

Her fear flooded through her chest. The guard was headed in their direction.

"You got this." Arie whispered to her. The words rolled off his lips so softly that she couldn't even hear his breath between words.

Just like textbook, the guard bent down and squinted into the cage. He reached for his belt.

Raine held her breath. A bright light illuminated their faces. She reached up and shielded her eyes with the back of her hand.

The guard grunted as he clicked his key into the steel lock and turned it.

Arie moved forward and used his arm to push Raine to the back of the cage.

She looked straight past Arie and into the eyes of the guard.

He stared straight back at her.

There was no turning back now.

The guard reached out and grabbed for Arie's throat, but the boy was quicker. He leaped out and tucked the man's head in a headlock.

Without thinking twice, Raine worked her way out of the cage, struggling with the fabric of her gown.

Everything was a blur. In her peripheral vision, she saw other inmates squirming. The faint sound of screaming, yelling out, and rattling the metal cages threatened to distract her as she tried to concentrate. She focused on this man that was keeping them locked up and doing terrible things for reasons she couldn't fathom.

Arie needs me!

While Arie was choking him, the guard had one arm clutching Arie's, with the other by his side.

She was about to leap forward onto the guard, when she caught a glimpse of the baton from his hip as he whipped it out with his free hand.

"No!" Raine shouted as the guard brought the baton upward and smashed it on Arie's forehead. She saw Arie's eyes roll up into the back of his head and he dropped to the floor.

She fell to her knees.

The guard transferred the baton to his other hand and swiftly locked it back on his belt, pulling something else out.

A gun.

"Don't move."

Raine froze as she held her breath, wide-eyed, staring down the barrel of the gun, on her knees. The sounds of the screams and banging on cages diminished as a cold, echoing silence fell.

Her lip quivered as she watched the guard pick up Arie under his arm with one hand, and move him into the cage. His cage. He locked the door and turned his attention back to Raine, keeping the gun pointed at her the entire time.

"Up against the wall." His commands were calm, quiet, and chilling, in spite of the fact he was just attacked and clearly out of breath. His full attention was on her, and nowhere else in the room. It was as if none of the other cages in the row even existed. "I said—"

He didn't have to say it again. Raine turned away from him and put her arms above her head in surrender. If Arie couldn't take him, she couldn't. And with a gun pointed at her head, it wasn't even worth trying.

She hated his breath on her neck as he grabbed her wrists and secured them down at the small of her back. She heard the clink of metal as he cuffed her. He grabbed the handcuffs from the middle and pulled her back.

"I'm not going back in there?" she asked in a whimper.

He didn't answer.

She already knew the answer.

The guard guided her down the row towards the door. And the haste at which he guided her told her that he hadn't been coming for Arie to begin with. He'd been coming for her.

There were two sets of double doors in the warehouse. The ones she entered through when she was first brought here, and another set on the other side. The latter doors were the ones that Arie and the blonde haired girl came through when they were brought back.

Raine was taken through the second set of doors. She hadn't seen this part of the prison yet. This hallway was identical to the other, low and lit with Edison bulbs. There were doors at odd distances, creating a pattern that didn't make sense. Her eyes were focused on the end of the hallway, where she tried to catch a glimpse of the set of stairs Megan reported.

She wouldn't get the chance to see if they were there or not, because the guard turned her, unlocked a door, and pushed her through.

She fell into a room. Familiar concrete floors and walls. This room was almost empty, her eyes fell upon the single bed in the corner. It had a black wrought iron frame, and tan sheets. Across the room were a table and two chairs.

She looked into the guard's face before she was forced away from him. He wasn't the one that did her intake, though his face was familiar. He was the other guard, the one that was standing in the door, taking the commands of the leader. She remembered him distinctly because she'd made a point to memorize their faces. This was the man that refused to make eye contact with her, and refused to even look at her while she undressed. He was respectful, if it could be called that. She deemed him as "the nice one," if that was possible either.

He turned her to face the wall and his fingers fumbled with the cuffs. Oddly enough, she felt the metal on her wrists slacken, and the handcuffs fell to the floor. He bent down and picked them up. She looked over her shoulder to see him attaching them back to his belt. When he saw her looking at him, his eyes flicked around before he spoke. "On the bed."

Every muscle in her body tensed. From deep within, the anxiety rose up and out of its hiding place. Her biggest fear was before her. Loss of control. Loss of... options. She could fight. She could thrash about and make it hell for him.

Instead, she just put one foot in front of the other, and walked towards the corner of the room. She took her time swiveling around and sat down on the creaky bed, avoiding his gaze.

"I'm sorry I have to do this," he whispered as he walked to the table.

Her ears pricked as she heard him drag the chair from the table to the door. She looked up to see him stepping up onto the chair, and adjusting a button on a black box above the door. It was a camera.

He turned it off.

SEVEN

Two Weeks Ago

She misted the cleaner down on the wood grain floors of her studio, and followed behind it with a paper towel. Yoga was done barefoot, and she was always on top of keeping things clean before the next session. The lights were still dim, and she had just unplugged the diffuser that let out scents of lavender and chamomile. A few women from the all women's pi-yo—Pilates mixed with yoga—session were still trickling out of the room.

"Should I put my mat over there on the shelf?"

Raine looked up at the door to see a timid young girl with curly red hair standing in the doorway holding her purple mat. She smiled at the girl and finished sweeping up the corner. "You can go ahead and take that with you, Lila. Thank you for coming to class today. It was a pleasure having you."

"It was so much more fun than my last experience with yoga." She laughed. "I'll definitely come again."

"That's great to hear. Remember, we do women's groups on Tuesday and Thursday nights, but you're welcome to come anytime." She walked up to her and held the door open. "Have a great night."

Lila nodded, and left through the door of the waiting room to catch up with her friends, who waited for her in the small, makeshift, parking lot.

Raine smiled to herself again before she turned and headed back into the studio. She walked up to the shelf and straightened the blankets so all the fringe was facing towards the wall.

The door shut behind her. "Marcus, I thought you decided to take off—" She spun around and stopped dead in her tracks.

"Disappointed it's me?" Troy asked with sly grin pasted across his lips.

She shrugged, and turned back to the blankets. "What do you want?"

Troy stepped closer to her. "Now that's not a very professional way to speak to your colleague, is it?" His voice was just above a whisper.

She turned towards him and crossed her arms.

He reached forward and grabbed a mat from the shelf.

"I just organized those!" she protested.

He turned away from her and made his way to the center of the floor.

"What are you doing?"

"I want a session."

"I'm done for the day."

He looked up at her, all traces of his grin gone. His mouth was thin and straight. "One of the perks of working in an office, that I *own*, is that I get to observe and experience the services that my colleagues are offering to clients."

"Sounds like a load of bullshit. Blackmail."

He stifled a laugh. "You think *this* is blackmail? I can show you blackmail, if that's what you want. Now just get up there and lead the damn yoga."

She hesitated. He technically could kick her out of the office. She wasn't paying rent. She wished she'd pushed the matter of a written agreement that said she had the right to stay there rent-free. Without the legal documentation, she couldn't protest. *All he wants is a lesson right? How hard can that be?*

Being alone with him in the room was constricting. Her radar was going off, and she already had an uneasy feeling. Regardless, she reached forward and grabbed her mat. "Take off your shoes, Troy. Nobody walks on my floor with shoes on." Her clean floor. Her eyes glazed over. She walked over to the diffuser and plugged it back in, the scent of lavender and chamomile puffing back into the air. She inhaled deeply into the mist and her muscles relaxed to her core. She thought about turning on some binaural beats or ocean waves, but he didn't deserve it. She preferred the silence. The silence made time feel slow, and his short attention span wouldn't last long.

"I can take off more than my shoes if you'd like." His words flicked off his tongue.

She ignored the comment and turned away from him. One side of the wall was completely mirrors, like a dance studio. Raine designed the room this way, because she liked having a reflection while exercising. Her students were able to see mistakes and adjust their poses.

She went through a series of heart opening poses, starting in the standing position. Working her way through stretching towards her toes, she moved into plank position, then up dog, and into down dog. Down dog was a resting pose, which gave opportunity to check in with the body. She rested both hands on the floor with her butt pointing at the ceiling. She felt the stretch deep in her hamstrings as she pedaled her feet back and forth. She loosened her neck and shoulder muscles, and took this opportunity to look up at the mirror to view her pose. In her peripheral vision, she looked back at Troy, who was in plank position, essentially a pushup held in place.

He stared directly back at her, smirk on his face. "Nice ass."

She fell out of down dog, spun around, and crossed her hands over her chest. "Enough," she said. Anger rose up in flames, licking her insides.

He laughed sheepishly. "What?"

"You're sexually harassing me, Troy. I'm sick of it. Enough."

"Oh get over it, you know you like it."

"I don't."

He got up and walked towards her.

She put her hands up to block him. "You don't want a yoga session. You want to harass me. You already crossed the line before we even started this, and I won't let it go any further." She tried to keep her voice from shaking. She was mostly an introvert, and it was hard for her to stick up for herself. But she wanted it to stop, and nobody was going to do it for her, she needed to take control herself.

She'd lived in the Bay area alone for a while. With her family back in Ohio, she learned to make it on her own. And when she stayed in San Francisco after college, she chose to make it on her own *without* help. She needed to stick up for herself.

"So you'll give it to Marcus, but not me? C'mon Raine."

She exhaled, infuriated. "What I do in my personal time is none of your business."

He laughed. "It's my business when there's a conflict of interest." His eyes were amused and his lips parted, revealing the gap in between his front teeth.

"There's nothing wrong with me being in a relationship—or seeing, whatever you want to call it, another colleague. Where does it say that in this hypothetical rule book you've invented?"

"I just don't like it happening around the office, okay?"

"I thought we were good at hiding it." Her cheeks burned.

"Clearly not."

"So, what then? If I don't have sex with you, you want me to leave the practice?"

Troy didn't answer. "You don't... No, that's not it."

"Are we done here? Why didn't you just come out and say something in the beginning? Why go through this charade?" Her voice trembled and she steadied it again.

"Because I wanted to look at your ass in those tight pants."

"Get the hell out," she spat.

He turned and leaned down to grab his shoes, and headed for the door.

She stood in front of the mirror with her arms crossed, watching his reflection.

He made it to the door, opened it, and left without looking back.

When the door slammed shut, Raine slipped down to the floor and allowed her eyes to well up and over. Her shoulders shook as she cried silently to herself, curled up in a ball.

What am I supposed to do? she asked herself, as she listened to the soft hiss of the lavender from the diffuser.

Raine looked down at her phone in her lap before she slipped it back in her purse, slung over the back of the chair. It'd taken her twenty minutes to get from her office to the coffee shop. She sat at a two-person table with her cup of sweet ginger green tea steaming on the table.

As she pulled her hair up and weaved strands into a French braid, she relaxed to the ambient sounds of the shop around her. She closed the braid at the bottom with a hair tie from her wrist. Clattering dishes were being washed in the back of the cafe. The barista behind the counter made small talk with a customer as they whirled the milk under a screaming steam wand. The smell of cinnamon hung in the air. The door behind her jingled as it opened and shut behind her.

"Girl, you know I'm always up for a coffee date!"

Raine flipped around to see her friend bouncing towards her. Melita was a ray of sunshine coming towards her as she opened her arms to embrace her.

"I got you your almond milk latte." Raine pointed to the mug across the table from her tea, the one with the rosetta latte art swirled on the top of the milk.

"You didn't have to do that—you're so sweet!" She smiled with her pearly white teeth, her cheekbones high and cheerful as the outside edges of her eyes crinkled with her smile.

"Of course!" Raine sat back down at the table and lifted her own mug up to her lips, sipping the hot liquid.

"So what's going on?" Melita asked as she slipped her jacket off her arms and draped it on the chair behind her. She re-situated the tan beanie on top of her wild, wavy hair. "That boy treating you right?" she teased.

Raine's smile slipped and she stared into her tea.

"Raine." Melita leaned across the table and placed a hand on top of hers.

"I got into a pretty bad situation with Troy at work today."

"That prick? What'd he do now?"

She heaved a sigh. "He really crossed the line this time. He's basically harassing me on a regular basis now." She told her friend about the yoga session situation she'd just experienced.

"That's horrible. Can't you do something?"

"Who am I supposed to report it to? He owns the building. He could kick me out at any time."

"Raine. You are a damn good psychologist with a freakin' doctorate and enough credentials for any office to take you."

Raine smiled. "Thank you. I really love having the freedom to run the practice the way I like it, without having to answer to somebody. I agree. I don't want to have to put up with this. But I can handle it."

"You shouldn't have to though, girl. That's awful. It's your workplace. You have a right to feel safe there.

You help empower people and help them find clarity in their lives. You need to take care of yourself as well. You practice yoga there. How are you supposed to honor your practice if you have a coworker constantly trying to get in your pants?"

The phrase made her laugh. She reached into her mug and pulled out the tea ball, then dropped it on the saucer underneath the cup. Some of the liquid seeped out, puddling the saucer.

"I'm serious."

"I know. Thank you, Melita. You always know what to say."

"What about Marcus? Have you told him what's been going on?"

Raine was silent again. "I have."

"And he hasn't jumped the guy?"

"Honestly? I think he thinks I'm imagining it."

"How the hell could you be imagining something like this? Uh-uh. Nope. You tell *that* guy to beat it too."

She laughed. "Well I didn't tell him what happened tonight, but I will. Marcus and I have just been good friends for such a long time, it's hard for me to get into the mindset that we're in a relationship now. I mean... I don't even know if I want that. Marcus and I have built such a strong foundation as friends. He's like home to me. What if something happens and we break up and I lose him?" She sipped her tea. "I know I should have thought about that before we hooked up, because that just leads men to wanting more, but, I don't know. I just want to keep it casual, you know?"

"So, you don't want to be with him because you don't want to lose him?" Melita asked.

They laughed together.

Raine brought her hand up to her forehead. "I've confused myself now."

"I get you, though. Don't let him pressure you into anything you don't want. Tell him to back off. Tell him you like hanging out as friends, but don't make it more confusing either. None of that friends with benefits shit, you know? Guys never understand the rules of that."

"You've got a point." They laughed again.

She fumbled with the tea ball on the side of her mug. "In all seriousness though, I have to have the conversation with him about all of this."

"I think he'll understand, girl. But hey, we should plan to do something soon. My family is having a big party next weekend. You should come. You know how huge and crazy my family is, and when we have quinceañeras and backyard parties, it's always a blast. You need to relax a little."

"I don't know... I love your family, Melita, you know that, but I'm not feeling very social as of late." She side smiled across the table.

"I understand. We could do something else to get you out. We could go hiking in Muir Woods across the bay?"

"Actually, I'd really love that. Thank you."

"Good. It's a date! Do you want a cookie or something from the pastry case? I could use a snack. I'll buy this time."

Raine sighed and moved her mug over. "I would love a snack right now." She smiled at her friend, the small cure to her terrible day.

EIGHT

Raine watched the guard turn off the camera. If she was her friend Melita, she would kick him in the balls right now. She smirked at the thought, but quickly wiped it away before he could see the emotion playing on her face.

He stepped down from the chair and walked back over to the table, unbuckling his belt and dropping it there. He turned to her.

"Please," she pleaded. "I'll listen to what you have to say. Please don't hurt me." She wasn't sure what was about to happen, but if it was something he didn't want recorded, it couldn't be good.

He walked up to the bed and sat down next to her. "Listen. I'm not going to hurt you. I turned the camera off because he's watching and I don't want him to see or hear what I'm about to tell you. He's always watching." The guard's demeanor had completely changed. His hands trembled in his lap.

She turned toward him and stared into his face. His eyes were sunken and darted around the small room. He showed all possible signs of an anxiety attack. She felt a deep sense of empathy towards him, and nearly forgot about the situation she was in. She reached up and put her hand on his arm to comfort him, though she couldn't fathom exactly why.

"Listen. I'm sharing this with you because I feel like you are our only chance of possibly escaping. I've been watching since you got here. You aren't like the others. You might have a chance."

He spoke so fast she found it hard to keep up. *OUR only chance of possibly escaping? Not just mine?* "Breathe. In and out. Long deep breaths for me, okay?" She worked him through it. "Tell me again. What's going on? Who's always watching?"

"We call him the Warden. I've never seen him. I just follow orders."

She tried to absorb the information without reaction. She'd get overwhelmed and lose control if she allowed herself to react.

He spoke again, "Look at me. You're the one locked up and you're sitting here comforting me."

She closed her eyes a moment. She couldn't help it. "It's just my nature."

"I know. That's why we're here. Listen. We don't have much time so I have to explain this quickly, okay? You need to keep up."

She nodded, waiting for the worst.

"One minute I was fishing off the dock, the next, I'm in a room with a massive headache. I'm thrown this guard uniform and told that I have to play the role of the guard."

"Wait—" It sounded all too familiar. She too, was in her normal life, doing things she'd normally do. Then she woke up here. There was evidence she'd been drugged. But what was she doing before she got here? This guard remembered he was fishing before he was taken. Why couldn't she remember exactly what had happened to her? She'd thought she was in some sort of state facility at first. And it enraged her even more that the head of this operation manipulated her into thinking she was a murderer. That everyone around her was a murderer.

"No, listen. We aren't given any rules on how to do this. But here's the thing. I can't leave. I'm being held here against my will."

"Then why do you do it?"

"I have no choice. I've got—" He choked up. "I've got a baby girl at home. She just celebrated her fourth birthday. And a wife. I want out. I'm a prisoner here just as much as you."

She narrowed her eyes. "But you wear *that* uniform. Not this one."

"If I don't perform the duties I think a guard is supposed to perform, my family is in danger. And that, to me, is me doing exactly what I need to survive and keep my family safe. Just like you."

She nodded. "Do you know much about this place?"

"Us guards call it Altruism Prison. Sort of like Alcatraz… in the bay."

"Wait, are we still in San Francisco? The Bay area?" She realized she had no clue where the prison was even situated.

"I have no idea. I'm not allowed out, just like you. There are no windows."

"Where do you sleep?"

"Guards quarters."

"How many of you are there?"

"Four that I know of. Two day, two night."

"Why call it Altruism Prison?"

"We have this theory that the man who's built this whole thing thinks he's doing it for the greater good. He's taken all these people off the street that have murdered others. Have you-have you murdered someone?"

Her breath caught in her throat. She felt the guilt rise from the pit of her gut, all the way up through her limbs. "I mean... not directly. No. I didn't. I didn't kill anyone."

The guard looked up at the camera. "We've been too long." He got up and walked back to the chair under the camera.

"Wait, what do we do? What's the plan? You're the guard, you have to have keys and such to all the rooms. You could be a big help—" She caught a glimmer in his eye. *How do I know I can trust him? What if he's playing double agent right now?* She pursed her lips.

Before he stepped up on the chair, he walked back over to her. "I'm going to unbutton my pants to make it look like I had a reason to turn off the camera, okay?" he asked her.

She nodded, looking from the camera back to him. He was unbuttoning his pants and zipped them open. "I'm sorry I have to do this—"

"Do wha—" Before she could finish her sentence, she took a blow to the head. She bit the inside of her cheek and blood sprayed from her mouth as she fell back on the springy, creaky bed. She wasn't entirely knocked out, and the pain in her jaw surfaced quickly. She reached up to touch the spot, when another blow struck right in between her eyes.

It knocked her out cold.

NINE

"**R**aine?"

She heard her voice called from the end of a tunnel. It was both familiar and unfamiliar at the same time. Her eyes fluttered open to the view of the metal ceiling. She heaved a massive sigh. She was hoping that maybe one of these times, she'd wake up back home. After all, she'd gotten here waking up after unconsciousness.

She was beginning to lose track of time, especially because of the lack of windows or natural light. She couldn't be sure whether it was night or day outside, there were only the controlled lights inside the warehouse.

As she lay alone in the cage, recognizing her surroundings once more, thoughts of the small room with the camera flooded back to her.

He was forced to play that role. Were the other guards forced as well?

She didn't know how to feel or what to do with her emotions. Her head pounded. Was that guard on this so-called Warden's side, or not? If not, why did he knock her out? Why did he leave her back in the cage?

She sat up and leaned on the wall that was closest to Arie's cage.

She thought she'd heard somebody calling her name again, though weaker this time. *Arie.* It was Arie. "Hey… " she breathed. Her voice was hoarse, exhausted.

"What happened, did they hurt you?"

"Mm… " She didn't even have the energy to respond.

She wanted to blurt out everything she'd learned during her time with the guard, but the memory of the camera came back. Were there cameras watching them right now? There had to be. There were probably cameras in every cage, down every row. Somebody, the Warden, was watching their every move. The Warden knew that Arie and Raine were put in the same cage together. He must have sent the guard after them. He must have expected the guard to punish her.

The thought was chilling. She wouldn't be able to tell Arie anything that had happened. At least not right away. "Are *you* okay? When I was taken away… you, you had been hit and thrown into your cage." She formulated each word carefully, as she stretched her jaw back and forth, trying to coax it back to working for her. After that blow to the jaw, everything felt bruised. The blood in her mouth still gave off a copper taste.

"I'm okay. I'm always okay. I get knocked around a lot."

Despite the situation, there was a boyish charm in his words. He was the type of guy that gave authority a run for their money. And he paid for it. But it was obvious he knew it, and didn't quit. "Tell me about your life outside of here. What do you do?" He asked.

The question startled her. "I'm a psychologist."

"Damn!"

That made her laugh. "What? After I graduated college, me and two guys I graduated with opened a co-op office where I do clinical therapy."

"So you're the real deal then?"

"What do you mean?"

"You deal with monsters all day?"

It was true. She'd dedicated her life to studying the human mind, and the human mind was a terrifying place to be. Not just that of others, but to study and see what the potentialities of her own thoughts were as well. "I think it has to do with a lot of factors. Humans aren't all innately bad. There's a lot of good. A lot of just amazing emotions and sensations."

There was a silence between them and she heard a fan turn on in the distance. There were always ambient sounds in the warehouse: vents, mechanical clanging, and alarms. It was never completely silent. For this she was grateful. She wasn't sure if she'd be able to deal with the silence, with only her screaming thoughts to keep her company. Of course right now she had Arie, and he was better company than any. "What do you do?" she asked. She reached up and massaged her tender jaw.

"I work with animals. I was studying to be a vet tech, but dropped out. Animals are much better than people."

"So if you dropped out, what'd you end up doing?"

"Well, I run a shelter in Palo Alto."

"A shelter?"

"Don't worry. It's a no-kill shelter. People always ask that, but I don't understand how shelters like that can still exist anymore. I could never do or endorse that."

"So you don't kill animals, but... you kill people?" Her sentence was staggered. Even though she was almost confident that nobody locked in one of these cages was a murderer, especially after her talk with the nice guard, she still had to ask. She bit her bottom lip as she leaned closer to his wall.

"I've killed someone—"

She inhaled.

"-just as much as you've killed someone."

Guilt ripped at her insides. *What a stupid question to ask.* "So you just take care of them?"

"Yeah. I just go around and get dogs and cats off the street mostly. Find their homes if they already have one. Find them homes if they don't. Feed them and give them a place to sleep."

"That's admirable." She put her hand up against the wall of her cage. Even though there was concrete between them, the divider was thin enough to hear through, and since the doors of the cages were bars, their voices carried.

Raine was careful to keep her voice low so she didn't disturb others. "I have a dog. She's my best friend. I miss her. It's just us two at my place. I hope somebody is able to feed her." She felt a tinge of sadness. "I have no idea how long I've been here."

Arie sighed loudly on the other side of the wall. "What's her name?"

"Viona. She's a mutt. You know, one of those scary looking protective dogs that people are afraid of when you walk by them. But she's a scaredy cat. She'd cuddle with a robber."

"You've got one waiting back at home. And you're her whole world. I've got thirty."

That sentence gripped her. "I'm sorry, Arie," she whispered, though she wasn't sure he heard her. "Sitting in here, I've been thinking about maybe some of the things in my life that I've done... that might have led me here."

"Don't do that. You'll drive yourself insane. And you know about insane."

Man, wait until I tell him about the Warden, she thought, remembering her conversation with the nice guard. "No. I do think I've, in a way, self prophesied myself into this exact point of my life."

"Okay. We've got time. Let's hear it."

"Well I'm thinking back to my first semester of college." She hesitated briefly and then recounted that moment in her life that changed her mode of thinking for all the years after.

Eight Years Ago

Raine clutched her red Solo cup, her oversized sweater covering half her hands. She sat on the lumpy couch, watching some fresh-faced guys tossing a ping-pong ball across the dinner table, engaged in an avid game of beer pong.

"Hey, hellooo. Earth to Raine."

She snapped out of it and looked over at her date, her roommate Maggie. "What did you say?"

"You into one of them or something?" she asked.

"Ha! No, I was just spacing out. I'm not really into parties all that much. You know I just came to make sure your ass doesn't do something you'll regret."

"Aw, if I don't do something I regret, then it's no fun." They both laughed.

"You want another drink?" she asked Maggie, her blonde-haired, blue-eyed roommate from Portland who made friends so easily. Raine had met her the day she moved into their closet-sized dorm room. She and her parents had been building a bed loft when Maggie waltzed in with her rolling suitcase. She hadn't brought her parents. She'd already claimed her independence. The reason Raine's parents had come with her was that she had been their first child to go off to college, and it was halfway across the county.

She filled Maggie's red cup with another ladle of boozy punch. She added some to her own cup, but only filled it halfway. Even though it was her first semester of college, and she wasn't of drinking age, she thought a little bit couldn't hurt. She realized her mistake when the room started spinning, and her movements were slower than her brain. She wouldn't let it go any further since she had class in the morning.

When she walked back into the family room, she held the two cups between the fingers of one hand, and fanned her face with the other, to rid herself of the smoky fog in the air. She was careful not to spill.

As Raine plopped herself down on the couch, Maggie inhaled through a metal mouthpiece attached to a tube, a device that looked like some kind of urn from Morocco. When she was finished, she shoved the mouthpiece into Raine's face.

"Naw, I'm okay." She passed it to the guy sitting in a lawn chair on her other side.

"C'mon. It's just a hookah. It's not weed or anything." Maggie laughed, and looked around the circle at the group for approval.

"Yeah, that's the OTHER room," one of the guys joked.

"I know." She shrugged and then laughed into her cup as she took another sip.

The guy in the lawn chair blew smoke in her direction as he shoved the hose and mouthpiece back at her.

What's it matter? It's only one time. She looked up at Maggie, and then took the mouthpiece from the guy. She raised it to her lips, and inhaled the blueberry-flavored tobacco. At the top of her drag, a cough escaped her lips, and she exhaled the smoke out into the room. She looked up, but it seemed like nobody was watching her. She passed the mouthpiece to her left again and nestled back in her chair.

It wasn't long after she was whispering in Maggie's ear that she wanted to go back to the dorms. She was ready to go home.

"Let me drive you!" Maggie shouted over the loud music that played through a built-in stereo system in the house.

"Naw, it's okay. It's not that far. I love walking. Anyway, it's a nice night out. I don't want to make you leave the party."

"Are you sure?"

"Yeah! I'll be fine."

"Then text me when you get back home, okay?" Maggie asked, squeezing Raine's arm.

"Okay, okay!" she laughed, and wrapped her arms around Maggie for a hug. "Don't stay out too late. You know we have Communications at eight tomorrow morning. I'm not going to take notes," she joked.

"Fine, be that way!" Maggie hugged her back, and then she twirled around and went back into the smoke, joining a few other laughing girls that Raine had never met. Maggie had such a way of making friends quickly. It's like she didn't care who the person was or what background they were from, she could always find something in common with them. Raine vowed to come out of her shell a little more, and learn how Maggie managed to be so outgoing. She could learn a thing or two from her.

She closed the front door behind her and took off down the steps of the townhouse, passing a couple making out on the stairs. She hoped her oversized sweater was enough to keep her warm in the brisk, San Franciscan fall night, but the wind was biting and it cut straight through her black leggings. She slung her crossbody purse diagonally across her chest, securing her phone in the front pocket of the bag. As she took off down the road, she thought about how proud she was that she had enough self-control to leave a party early. She would get back to the dorm and get a head start on sleeping, so she could be awake and feel good in the morning for class.

She focused on the connecting pools of light from the streetlights. She turned out of the neighborhood and crossed the street onto the campus. The party house was in the neighborhood right outside campus, so there was no need for her to hop on public transportation to get back to the dorm.

As she walked, Raine saw a student on his bike zoom past her, and a group of giggling girls across the street turned the corner and out of sight. She continued walking straight.

She tucked her hair behind her ear and looked up, passing a black car parked against the curb to her right side. As she walked by, she heard the door click. She looked around to see what buildings were nearby, wondering why somebody would be there on a Sunday night, but she kept her head down and minded her own business. She reached up and rubbed at her eyes. They were beginning to itch with tiredness, and once again she was happy that she'd decided to leave the party when she did. She looked up from the sidewalk again to gauge the distance from where she was to the crosswalk, and sensed a presence behind her.

A looming shadow covered her.

She looked over her shoulder, but it was too late.

Somebody very strong wrapped their arms around her and jerked her feet out from underneath her. She yelped out into the night air and threw her elbow back, hitting something hard. Shock waves from her funny bone prickled down her arm. She must have hit a belt buckle. She tried to turn her head to see the face of the person who was groping her, but the man shoved her down by the back of her neck. Her chin was forcefully tucked into her chest, choking her, and making it harder for her to breathe. As she gasped for air and clawed behind her miserably, the man dragged her, which at one hundred and ten pounds and petite frame, wasn't hard to do. He dragged her towards the black car she passed moments before.

Raine thrashed around, but it was no use. It was almost too easy for the man to get her to the car. He had reached the vehicle and was fumbling with the handle of the door when Raine heard a shout coming from the other side of the crosswalk.

"Hey!"

The person forcing her into the car froze.

"Raine? Is that you?"

As she heard her name, she was dropped to the pavement. She landed on her hands, coughing and gasping for air. She lifted her head to try and see who had grabbed her, but all she saw was a face full of exhaust as the car peeled out and tore off down the road.

Terrified tears almost overcame her, and she stayed on the pavement a moment before looking up to see a beefy guy kneeling by her side, out of breath.

"I thought it was you! Did you know that man?" he asked.

Raine shook her head.

The man kneeling beside her in a football jersey and shorts was a kid from one of her psychology classes. He must have recognized her from across the street.

"Thank... thank you," she breathed.

"We need to tell someone about this. Like now-"

"No!"

He stood back, dumbfounded. "You were just assaulted. On a university campus."

"I don't want to deal with it. Please. Just, please let it go."

They sat together on the pavement a moment under the spill of the streetlamp. "Can I walk you to wherever you want to go then?"

"I'd really like that," she whispered. She wasn't sure what to think. He'd just saved her life. But she'd read and seen on social media about all the cases of university harassment that slipped under the radar. She didn't want to kick up the sand in a new school that she'd worked so hard to get into. She'd be told it was an isolated incident. Or she could get in trouble for underage drinking, or for going to that party with upperclassmen to begin with. The university might tell her that she was just another girl trying to get attention. She didn't want to mess up her chance at a reputable degree. She couldn't tell her roommate, because Maggie would be mad at her for leaving the party early. Maggie would say if she hadn't left early it never would have happened. She couldn't tell her parents, because they'd be on the next flight out here, or make her come home. They'd obviously make her report it. They'd be mad at her for walking at nighttime alone.

She'd thought she was safe. She hadn't been aware of her surroundings. *I wasn't paying attention to every detail around me as I walked alone. My carelessness caused this terrible thing, or almost really terrible thing, to happen. It's really all my fault.*

The football player from her introductory psych class put out his hand for her and she took it, using his strength to pull her to her feet.

She was shaking all over, made worse by all the thoughts going through her mind.

"That was messed up, man," the guy said as they walked next to each other down the street she'd been dragged down just moments before.

Raine couldn't keep her knees from trembling uncontrollably as she readjusted her purse and wiped away the tears. *One foot in front of the other.* They walked until they got to the door of her dormitory.

Without even looking her hero in the face she mumbled, "Thank you so much."

"Anytime. You sure you're okay?"

She nodded her head and fumbled in her purse for her ring of keys and building fob.

"Okay. Hey, I'll see you in class."

She nodded once more, and unlocked the front door.

When she got into her room, locked the door, and crawled into bed in the same clothes she'd been wearing all day, she pulled out her phone. Her fingers shook as she texted Maggie:

Safe.

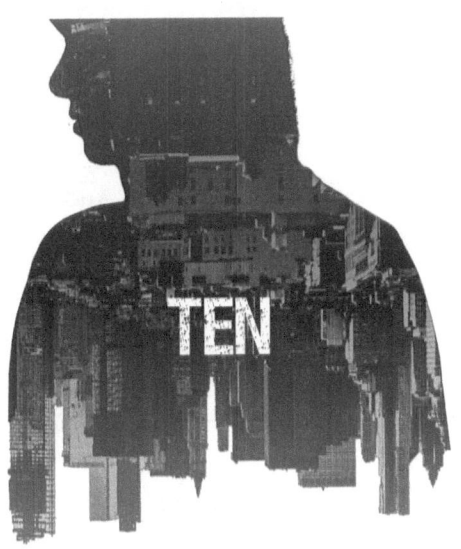

TEN

"So you never told anyone?" Arie asked.

She shook her head, and remembered that he couldn't see her. "I never did. And… " her voice cracked, "I've never told anybody that story before. But I can pinpoint that day as a pivotal moment in my life. After that, I was always looking over my shoulder. Anywhere I went, I'd formulate in my mind what I would do in specific situations. Like, if I was leaving the grocery store, what would I do if somebody was underneath my car, waiting to cut the tendon behind my ankle as I unlocked the door?"

"Damn." he breathed.

"I'm a psychologist. I help people every day with disorders like this. Paranoia. Anxiety. Things that get so bad that they impair your normal life. I help people sort this shit out all the time! But how am I supposed to be a good life coach, if I can't even handle my own anxieties and paranoia? How am I supposed to live a life where I'm constantly looking over my shoulder for that man in the black trench coat to come up behind me and grab me again, to take my life away?"

Arie remained quiet.

"I self prophesied getting taken. And look where I am now. This prison. It's a prison all right, but not legal by any means."

"I know."

"You know?"

"Well, isn't it obvious, Raine? Look at our cages. You think I think this is a government facility?"

"Well, no."

"It's just a matter of who, right? Just like in your story. You don't know who the man with the black trench coat was, do you, or the fact that maybe he wasn't wearing a black trench coat at all? Maybe your mind made that visual up as time went on, filling in the pieces that your memory failed to. In your original story, you never said you could even see what the man looked like."

"You're right. I hadn't thought about that before. But it's comforting, believe it or not, in this circumstance, to put a visual with the situation."

"I do that all the time here. I don't care who the unknown higher power is, running the place. All I see is the guards and how they treat me. To me, the guards are the face of why I'm in here."

Raine turned around on her knees and crawled towards the front of the cage. "Arie, come here. Come to the front of the cage." She heard a soft shuffling next to her. "I want to tell you something, but it has to be quiet, and it has to be quick." She saw his fingers stretching to her cage. "When I was taken away from here, a guard told me that-" She lowered her voice even more, "-that he was also here against his will. He doesn't remember what happened, just like me, but he knows that he has to follow commands from someone or there are consequences."

"The guards were kidnapped as well?"

"Yes."

"How do you know he wasn't just telling you that to get information out of you, to bring back to whoever's higher up?" he asked.

"The situation... I don't know. I just feel like I can trust the guy. Don't you find it strange, though? This is a bigger operation than we thought."

He was quiet for a moment, and then mumbled something.

Raine pushed her ear up against the cool bars. "Hm?"

"I just said... well the guards are the ones that enforce the punishment, therefore, they are the face of this madness for me. I don't give a shit that they have a higher up. That's their problem."

Raine pursed her lips. "That's valid, but we need a plan B. Because Plan A didn't work."

"While you were gone, Meg came and talked to me."

"What did she have to say?" Raine rubbed her eyes, sliding her hands over her forehead to her hair. *How is it that Megan has free rein of the prison? It doesn't make any sense. Arie trusts her but not the guard?*

"She said to hang tight. She's working on another plan. She's most of the reason that I keep sane here in this place. Look around you. Look at these people," he whispered.

Raine sighed. Megan's hope would have to do for now. At least someone was working on something. She placed her hand on her achy stomach, and looked out the bars into the row of cages. There were so many, though not all of them were occupied. The two guys she saw in the cages directly across from her rarely stirred. She always caught them sleeping or laying there lethargic. They were human, just like her.

Her first night here—who knows how long ago that was—she was told she was in a place for murderers. The more time that passed behind bars, the more slivers of truth she uncovered.

She leaned back in the cage.

The Warden. Ever since the guard told her about this authority, she couldn't stop thinking about the possibilities. She'd studied the human mind, in textbooks, clinically, and throughout her life. *Was* the guard telling the truth? Was there somebody else that was blackmailing him? Somebody who had the capability to kidnap all these people from their daily lives, and go unnoticed?

Though the more time that went by, the less likely it was that anybody would find her. Surely if she missed work at all, Marcus and Troy would be looking for her. She never missed a day of work.

Troy. The thought crossed her mind that set chills up her spine, jolting her. He had quite a bit of access to her. She'd let her guard down around the office, a place where he knew she was vulnerable.

Could Troy pull off an operation like this? She'd contemplated his mental state, which was a common and natural occurrence for her, someone who'd studied the human condition. The first step to learning psychology is to diagnose all those who are close.

Troy used to hang out in Marcus and Raine's study group when they were researching their dissertations.

When she and Marcus had the idea to open a practice together after they graduated, Troy was quick to jump on it.

She'd recognized misogyny early on in Troy. He'd undermine her when she'd answer one of the questions on their study guide. She just ignored it, finding him somewhat of a jealous person. He was the opposite of her, often loud and obnoxious. When she tried to hold a conversation with him, he'd talk over her and not wait for her response after asking a question. He carried himself with arrogance, an air that he was better than everyone.

She was aware of this going into practice with him, but Marcus said things would be different. They weren't, really.

She couldn't help but hate Troy more as she sat on the concrete of this prison.

Troy's not capable of an operation like this, she thought. Yes, surely the kidnapper, the Warden, had to have some sort of connection to her in her real life, but Troy wasn't organized enough to pull off something this elaborate, with so many people involved. *Was he?*

"So what happened when you were gone, Raine?" Arie asked from the other side of the wall.

"I told you. I had that conversation with the guard." She said.

"It's okay if you don't want to tell me."

"What are you talking about?"

"You were gone for so long. I'm thinking it had to be half a day."

She didn't like that thought. She didn't like feeling vulnerable, not knowing what happened to her, the fact that anything could have been done to her while she was unconscious. She even opted for Novocain over anesthesia when she had her wisdom teeth extracted. She couldn't stand the thought of being unconscious and not in control. "I don't know, Arie. I don't know what happened to me. I have these moments in time that are just blank. I can't even freakin' remember what I was doing before I woke up in this hellhole!" The walls on all four sides closed in on her in her mind. It was such a tiny space. She couldn't breathe. She couldn't get out.

"Breathe."

She heard his voice. *Why is he talking to me? Why does he even care? He's got Meg. He doesn't need me. I'm just slowing him down.* So many thoughts raced through her mind, hitting all the curves inside. She closed her eyes and breathed. Inhale. Exhale. That's all she had to do. Nothing else. Just inhale and exhale.

"Are you hungry?" he asked.

She opened her eyes and cupped her hands over her stomach. "I'm starving," she admitted.

"When you were gone, Meg brought us all some food. I wasn't sure if you'd get fed. I saved you some bread. Come to the front of your cage."

She was already there.

"See if you can reach." He slipped a piece of bread through the bars.

She reached to grab it, thought she had it, but dropped it on the floor. She stretched her fingers out the best she could, so far that she felt like she would almost rip her middle finger off, the longest finger, but she reached the bread.

As she leaned into the bars, the lock on the door snapped, and chinked to the floor.

"Did you get it?" he asked.

She froze as she looked down at the lock on the floor, then back up through the bars. The two guys across from her cage were either out cold, pushed to the back, or taken out. It was so dark in the warehouse, she couldn't tell.

She felt like she was in shock, all her muscles tense and shaky as she reached out and touched the door, pushing it forward. It creaked. "Arie," she said, almost inaudible.

"What's wrong?" He was at the front of his cage.

"It's unlocked." She finished pushing open the door and peered out, down the row both ways. She crawled out of the cage and grabbed the bread, bringing it up to her lips. Nothing tasted better in her entire life, and she closed her eyes, chewed it up, and swallowed. As her body felt the food going down her throat, her stomach grumbled. "Thank you," she whispered, finishing off the bread and feeling the lock on Arie's door with her fingers.

"How... ?" He gaped at her and clutched both hands around the bars in front of his face.

"You think the guard... is it possible he did it on purpose?" she asked, as she continued to finger his lock. "I can't get yours."

"You're just going to have to go."

"I can't, I don't know where to go."

"Go down. Find those stairs Meg was talking about."

"What if he sees me? The guard said he's always watching. I'm scared."

"Raine. Look at me. Be scared for your life. This is your chance."

"What if the consequences are worse?" She grabbed the bars he was holding and put her forehead up against the cage. "I can't leave without you, Arie." The urgency and panic in her voice was palpable.

"You have to give it a shot. You can do this. I believe in you. Hey. Look at me." He reached through the bars and tilted her chin up.

She came face to face with him, staring right into his stony, green-flecked, gray eyes.

"You are strong. Run. You can come back for me. If you're caught, give them hell."

Her lip trembled, and she nodded her head to show him that she understood.

He reached through the bars and ran his thumb down her cheek. "They got you pretty bad," he whispered. "You're bruised."

"You're pretty banged up yourself," she whispered back, observing his purple cheekbone and bloodshot eyes.

"You're strong willed. You can do this. You have to."

"I'll come back for you." And as much as she hated the thought of leaving him behind in the cage, she turned away. Her eyes had adjusted to the darkness. She slowly crept down the row of cages, her bare feet noiseless on the cold, damp concrete. They carried her down the same path she'd been dragged down before, towards the second set of double doors.

ELEVEN

Raine pushed her way through the darkness to the wall, moving like a ghost. She traced her hands along the oversized cement blocks. Standing still a moment, she listened for any signs of movement that sounded like it was outside of a cage. When she felt like the coast was clear, she heard the echo of footsteps. They were loud and booming, steel toed boots, pacing slowly up and down the row to her right. She wouldn't have to pass that row to get out, but she needed to move quickly, because she couldn't predict which way the guard would be headed.

There were two day guards and two night guards. Although she never knew when it was day or night, she had to assume that this was one of the night guards.

She looked over her shoulder, back at her cage. Without realizing it, she had closed the door behind her, so a guard wouldn't notice it ajar. Arie was still locked up. There was no time to think about that. She needed to go.

She crept down the wall to the double doors. Luckily, the door was ajar, though it wasn't open enough for her to slip through. She looked over her shoulder. She couldn't see the guard. She was going to have to pull open the massive steel door just a little bit to slip through, regardless of her petite frame. There was no other way. She'd already gone too far.

She clutched the door with both hands and tugged with all her strength. The rusty hinge made a terrible creaking sound, something that sounded like nails on a chalkboard, and she closed her eyes as she slipped through and threw herself up against the wall on the other side.

"It already time?"

She heard the booming, deep, throaty voice on the other side of the door, in the warehouse.

"I thought I still had another quarter of the shift?"

The voice was getting closer. The pounding of the guard's steel toed boots hitting the concrete floor echoed off her skull as she put her hand up to her mouth to quiet her breathing.

The footsteps stopped. There was a moment of painful silence.

"Hmph."

He was right on the other side of the door.

A moment later, footsteps echoed again. This time they were beginning to sound more and more faint.

She rested her hand down by her side and exhaled, looking down the long dimly-lit hallway. She tiptoed, looking into the corners to see if there were cameras. In this day and age, cameras were easy to hide, and surely they were everywhere. But she couldn't do anything except keep going.

There were doors on the right side of the corridor, since the warehouse covered most of the left.

She passed by the only familiar door—the one that she'd been in with the nice guard.

She recalled Arie telling her that Megan said the stairs were at the end of the hall. Of course she didn't know which end, but she had to choose.

Everything felt blurred as she ran her hand along the wall. She was exhilarated by her escape, yet everything was terrifying and closing in on her as she weighed the possibilities of the consequences. Desperation drove her, and she couldn't think of anything other than the fact that she had to keep moving forward.

When she reached the end, she placed her hands upon the steel. *Would it trip an alarm? Would it be locked? Could this door be the only thing keeping me from escaping?* She pushed her body into the door, swung herself inside, and leaned her back against it.

She was through it. It was almost too easy—too good to be true.

She looked ahead and, sure enough, just as she hoped, a staircase. It spiraled down. Her legs shaking, she took the stairs one at a time while hanging onto the railing for support. There was a breeze in the stairwell, and she felt a draft on her legs. She felt exposed and vulnerable in the gown, which was paper thin and clung to her skin.

As she went down, she wondered what to expect at the bottom. The anticipation reminded her of all the anxiety she'd felt in her life, derived from the paranoia she experienced every time she walked on the street alone, even in broad daylight.

Two Weeks Ago

Years had passed since she'd been dragged towards the black car on the side of the road. The scene played out again and again in her head as if it'd only just happened yesterday. The what-ifs. What if she'd stayed longer at that party? What if she'd been able to reach her phone in her purse faster? What if that football player that recognized her from class hadn't been there?

What if the man in the trench coat had gotten her into the car?

That moment shaped all of the moments that followed: when she'd gone to the grocery store. Leaving the office. Walking Viona.

It became a constant state of consciousness, awareness of her surroundings. Each day she studied other people's anxieties and paranoia. She taught people to overcome their fears, the fears that were impairing their daily lives and the comfort that was impaired by fear—even though she couldn't control her own.

She gathered up her papers and stuffed them in her laptop bag. She'd stayed too late at the office again, something that had become a common occurrence. The problem with owning her own practice was the fact that she had the ability to make her own appointments. Lately she liked the idea of sleeping in, so she scheduled her appointments in the afternoon. When she arrived to the office late, she stayed later. Though in any normal circumstance, that should have been fine. She had the right to stay late at her office if she wanted to, without feeling fear.

She made sure she turned off her office lights and closed the door. Marcus's office was closed, the light under the door turned off, and Sylvie had gone home for the day. She turned the two lamps in the reception area off and made her way to the door. A light beamed from a crack of an open door behind her. Troy's office.

She stood a moment, turned, and walked up to the door.

"If you're staying late, will you turn down the thermostat before you leave?" she asked.

He was hunched over his computer, hovering inches from the keyboard. He jerked up when she spoke, and his chest rose and fell quickly.

"Sorry, didn't mean to—did I interrupt something?"

"No. I'll get the thermostat." He went back into his crouched position at the keyboard.

Raine bit her lip and turned to leave, catching a glimpse of his elbow on the desk. He had deep crimson scratches across his arm. "Troy! You're bleeding." She squinted at the injury.

He turned from her, and swiped his other hand across the gouge, smearing the fresh blood. "Get outta here, Raine."

"What happened?" she pressed the matter.

He pushed his chair back abruptly and stood. He walked towards her.

She took a step back, out of the doorway.

"Nothing. I hit the edge of the cabinet. I'll get the thermostat." He held the door.

She nodded and turned. "See you tomorrow."

"Yeah, see ya."

Without looking back, she charged through the waiting room and out the door, turning to lock it behind her. She took off through the small parking lot that could fit only a few cars, and situated herself on the sidewalk.

When she didn't have to drive, she walked or took public transportation. If she could reduce her own carbon footprint even just slightly, she'd always take that route.

As she walked at a brisk pace, she was grateful she'd remembered to bring a scarf that day. She was used to the weather in the Bay Area, where she could wear a short-sleeved shirt but needed a scarf.

The leaves were changing, and the briskness in the fall air was biting. She couldn't help but think about the four scratches, equally spaced, on Troy's arm. That wasn't a cabinet. Those were from nails. Human nails.

She wanted to call Marcus and tell him what she'd seen, but she was walking home now and didn't want to be on her phone. She needed to be fully aware of her surroundings as she walked to the streetcar stop.

As she walked along the sidewalk, the street lamps just turning on for the evening, she caught a glimpse of a man up ahead walking towards her. He had broad shoulders, and wore a muscle tank and gym shorts.

He's just working out. She documented in her mind every detail about his appearance as if she had to give a police sketch in an hour. Grey tank, red gym shorts. Running shoes. Tube socks. Bronze skin. Broad shoulders. Ripped arms and shoulders. Buzzed head. Brown eyes? Maybe hazel, too far to tell. Narrow nose.

He was getting closer.

Her heart raced and she thought they'd made eye contact when she was trying to figure out the color of his eyes. She shifted her glance away.

No. Look him in the eye. When you make eye contact and acknowledge they are there, they are less likely to choose you as a victim, because they know you are aware.

As he approached her, she felt a numbing sensation run through her limbs. It was almost time.

She smelled sweat on the wind as he blew past her and continued on his workout down the road. She exhaled.

He'd passed. He hadn't even looked at her; had no interest in her.

She instantly internalized the feeling in the pit of her stomach. *This guy was just living his life, doing his workout.* She'd pegged him as a bad guy before she gave him a chance.

What's wrong with me? she thought and sighed. If she hadn't experienced what she had, would she be more trusting of humanity? Would she still feel that every person was out to get her?

She reached the F line streetcar and stood by the map, tapping her foot on the sidewalk, as an old woman holding her handbag sat on the bench.

As she ran her hand along the railing in the stairwell, she thought back to that moment. She'd had a right to be afraid of a strong, unfamiliar man coming towards her. Only he didn't do anything to harm her. And he only fueled in her the illusion of danger. Every incident like that made her feel like she was the one acting ridiculous.

And now she tried to live her life with caution and awareness, yet it didn't matter. Perhaps if she hadn't dreamt up all the possible situations that could happen to her, this never would have happened.

But look at me now. I was taken.

Her worst fear came true.

TWELVE

Raine stumbled down the last few steps and pressed her hands against the door at the bottom. She looked back up the stairs. *Only one floor down?* It was odd that there weren't any stairs leading down from this stairwell. Her eyes scanned the door, and her gaze landed upon the red glowing light of the EXIT sign.

As she laid her hands against the door, she tried to absorb the energy through the metal. Was her freedom there on the other side of the door? When she pushed it open, would the sun embrace her? Would it be another hallway? So far she'd been able to make it without being followed, and no alarms had sounded behind her. When she pushed through the door, would it trip an alarm *this* time?

There was only one way to find out.

She put one hand on the handle and the other against the metal. She turned the knob and leaned in with all her might.

No alarm.

She squinted into the white light.

She was definitely outside the prison. But she was not outside the building. She closed the door behind her, and grabbed hold of the handle from the inside to allow the latch to meet the frame without slamming.

She turned back around as her eyes finished adjusting and leaned back. She scanned the room.

Some sort of loft space? It was an open floor plan: family room straight into the kitchen, with a huge entertaining island in between, all white marble. She walked into the room, her bare feet chilly on the cold, white tile. She tried to swallow, her throat dry, her chest rising and falling in rapid motions.

The family room held a sofa with armchairs across from it, and a coffee table in between. She walked up to the couch and went to touch it, but thought twice. She felt dirty, like her fingers would stain the white furniture.

A large crystal chandelier hung above the furniture in the sitting area, and her eyes followed the beams of rainbow light from the sunlight through the windows hitting the crystals of the chandelier and scattering. *Windows!*

She scurried over to the floor-to-ceiling glass, feeling incredibly exposed, especially in her gown. She ran her hand along the sheer white curtains. The sun was blinding, and an immense pain erupted in her head from the bright light. She'd been in the dim, gloomy prison for who knew how long, and her eyes could not adjust. What she could see outside was a thick fog. Nothing but fog.

She made her way around the perimeter of the apartment, keeping her eyes peeled. Off to her left was a set of stairs that led up to a loft, no doubt the bedroom.

Where am I? she wondered. She was overwhelmed. Everything in her sight was clean, and pure, and beautiful. A complete contrast to the dark, cold, musty, uncomfortable prison she'd spent an unaccountable amount of time in. The prison. This place was directly underneath it.

As the realization hit her, her trance shattered into a million pieces and she nearly fell to her knees. How was it possible that this place was directly underneath the prison? So close to them, yet she'd been suffering in a cage where she couldn't even stand. Did the guards know about this place? Did Megan know about this place?

She stood still a moment. Only the ambient noise of the air vent spilled sound into the room. The rest was silent.

How do I get out, if the only door in here leads back up to the prison? She scanned the room again for any signs of an exterior door. The windows were sheets of glass, with no way to open them or hinge them upwards. She walked toward the kitchen. Not a single speck marred the white surfaces. She neared the large farm sink cut out in the counter and stopped dead in her tracks.

Sitting in the sink was a coffee mug. Used. Somebody lived here.

There was only one answer as to who. Someone that wasn't worried about keeping their doors locked. Mainly because the only visitors they'd ever have were behind a lock themselves.

She was a hundred percent certain that this was the home of a dangerous, dangerous person.

The Warden.

THIRTEEN

Her stomach sank into a fiery pit of rage as she eyed the coffee mug, a tiny pool of black liquid in the bottom of the cup. She imagined a man drinking the steaming mug with traces of hazelnut early this morning as if he weren't torturing people just on the floor above him.

As her thoughts drifted to who could be responsible, she remembered where she was. She'd escaped. She'd come into the loft through one door, and needed to find the way out.

There had to be a way out.

There was no way that the only escape could be up.

Raine looked over her shoulder before she grabbed the chrome handle of one of the kitchen drawers and pulled it open. Measuring cups, rubber spoons, and spatulas. She closed the drawer. Next, spoons and forks. Next, potholders.

"C'mon… " She reached around the dishwasher and pulled out another drawer. She stared into it before she reached in and grasped the handle of a four-inch, serrated knife.

Holding it up, she looked at her reflection in the blade: sunken, bloodshot eyes. Bruised jaw. Dry, cracked lips. She placed the tips of her fingers on her bottom lip.

As she stared at herself in the blade, she thought of what Arie must have been thinking as he touched her cheek through the bars. Just one look, one touch was enough to know how much he truly wanted her to escape.

And Marcus was probably searching for her right now. He was probably worried sick. He was a good guy. He was one of her best friends. They tried at the possibility of a relationship and it didn't feel right for her.

As she looked into the reflection on the knife, she half expected to see somebody standing behind her shoulder, but only the reflection of an exhausted, desperate girl stared back.

A door slammed.

She spun around and held the knife down by her thigh. There was nowhere for her to put it in the gown she wore. For a moment, she was frozen in the kitchen. Nowhere to go. White everything. Exposed.

She crouched down to the floor. The knife clattered on the ground and she held it up, realizing her hands were shaking like a dry oak leaf in the middle of fall. There was nothing to do but move. The noise came from down the hall that she hadn't had the chance to explore yet. Her only other option was to go back the way she came, though she wanted to do anything other than go back to the prison through those doors.

She scooted across the floor on her knees and the grout in the tile ripped into her kneecaps. The adrenaline circulating through her veins was enough to keep her hands steady, particularly the one with the knife, as she passed the refrigerator and rounded the corner. She peered down the hall. There was no movement. It was clear.

There were only two doors to choose from, both were closed. One was probably the bathroom, gauging the style of the loft. The other, the way out.

She opted for the door at the end of the hallway, the most logical one to be another set of stairs. Raine rose to her feet and tiptoed down the hallway, towards the slamming door she'd just heard.

What the hell am I doing? she asked herself as fear ripped at her insides, tearing through her stomach and nerves. The only thing driving her was the undying knowledge that there was absolutely no other choice. She'd gone in too deep.

She reached the door at the end of the hall, grabbed the knob with her free hand, and turned it as slowly as she could.

The best-case scenario would be that she made it to the other side of this door and could run down the flights of stairs to the bottom without being caught. She pulled the door back, and peered around it.

An empty room.

Four white walls. No windows. No other doors. No stairs.

Though something caught her attention immediately. It was the scent of creamy sandalwood, along with the lush floral heart of iris softened by fresh cut cedar wood, and it wafted from the room and drew her inside.

It was familiar. Comforting.

As she looked up into the corners of the room to try and find its source, the door slammed shut behind her. Raine dropped the knife to the floor with a clatter, just centimeters from her toes. She jiggled the doorknob, now locked.

"No!" She screamed at the top of her lungs. Her throat constricted.

The walls closed in. The panic set in.

She banged her fists against the door and screamed. "Let me out!" until her knuckles were swollen and bloody. When nothing came of that, she slumped down on the ground with her back against the door.

The familiar, comforting scent of the sandalwood triggered her senses again. *Why is it so familiar?* Sandalwood was used for anxiety, or a sleep aid.

Immediately, the source of the scent memory appeared clearly inside her head. It was so overwhelming it was almost sickening. Her head swirled. It was such a mild, calming, beautiful smell and he was using it against her.

She burned incense all the time in her office. She and her colleagues were each able to choose a scent that they preferred. She chose lavender and honey, a scent she often used in her diffuser in the yoga room. Marcus was partial to rose geranium. There was only one person in the office that burned sandalwood.

That person was Troy Batterman.

She was small. Helpless. Stuck in the role she was forced to play. What did Troy want with her? What did he want with all these people? How could he even do something like this? She'd noticed signs of anger in him, and she had an idea of the kinds of things he was capable of in his personal life, but she never realized it could or would amount to something like this.

There was no use expending any more energy in trying to escape the room. As she sat upon the cold floor, her bottom exposed in the thin gown, she looked at the tile and realized for the first time that there were vents in the surface. Four of them. That must have been the physical source of the scent pumped into the room. And just as she allowed the scent to take over her body, tingling through her anxious breathing, a new scent wafted from the vents and overwhelmed her. It was the strong stench of chemicals, also familiar. The scent she had traces of in her nostrils when she'd woken up to this nightmare. She pulled the gown up over her nose and mouth to try and shield herself from the anesthetic, but it was too late. The room grew foggy. Raine coughed, hacking up what felt like her lungs. She lost control of her limbs, her eyelids heavy. It was no use fighting. She had to… she couldn't keep her eyes…

FOURTEEN

Raine's consciousness came back before she opened her eyes. She heard movement above her head. There was pressure on both her wrists and her ankles, and a cool draft chilled her entire body. The memory of what had happened before the world went black came flooding back to her. She slowly opened her eyes and looked around.

She was still in the room at the end of the hall, though it wasn't empty anymore. She was lying on an elevated table, something similar to a massage table. Wide eyed, she moved her head back and forth to try and see what was happening. Her arms and legs were bound with leather straps that stretched to hooks on the walls.

And her gown had been removed. She lay naked and exposed on the cool leather table, helpless. She let her limbs relax, which relieved the pressure on her wrists and ankles. Tears of utter fear leaked out of her eyes and disappeared into her hairline. She sniffled and felt the familiar sting of chemicals in her nose.

"I've only let one other girl see who I am. She brought me comfort when I thought all hope was lost. But she's still a prisoner. And for that she will be punished." The voice had come from above her head, though she wasn't able to twist to see him.

"Megan," she croaked. "Is Megan here?" she asked. Silence. "Please don't hurt me." She squeezed her eyes shut.

"I get to be the one that asks the questions now." His voice was cold as he rounded the table.

She flinched at the sound of a scrape on leather, and opened her eyes to see the knife she'd acquired from his kitchen earlier dragged across the table by her side.

The knife! she screamed inside her head. She followed the line of the blade up the arm of her captor and into his face.

It was not Troy.

She was mostly relieved, but overwhelmed with fear and unresolved feelings, all at the same time.

The middle-aged man with thinning white hair glared down through the doubled barred nineties aviator frames.

She didn't know him. She didn't recognize his face.

"Lets not talk about Megan. Lets talk about you. You toy with people's minds all day long. You think you have the upper hand." As he spoke to her, he punctuated his words with the knife. "Because you've studied the brain doesn't mean you have any idea what's going on inside the minds of your play toys. I'm the smartest Warden there ever was. I've gotten all you murderers off the street for the greater good of the rest of humanity."

"I never killed anyone."

"Quiet!"

She shivered in her restraints at his outburst, which only pulled them tighter. She realized she was in some sort of mechanism. A trap. Just like one set for an insect or vermin. Quicksand. The more you struggled, the tighter the restraints. She couldn't move any more, or the straps would cut into her skin.

He leaned back and watched, then smirked as if he were proud of his work. Proud of his control.

Raine struggled inside herself to find the strength to figure out what to do next. She had a lot of training in how to deal with clients and patients who lost it. She'd been highly qualified to work with unstable people, people that needed help. That's what she did for a living. That's what she dedicated her life to. In order to survive this, she needed to look past fear and use her training.

This man was delusional. He needed help. She'd been told to shut up, but she wanted to try one last thing. "We can get through this. You are not alone," she breathed.

When he didn't respond right away, her mind took off, considering his possible reactions. She always thought the absolute worst until she got a response.

"Dr. Batterman used to say that. But he is not my friend. He was toying with my mind too, trying to make me take drugs, just like you do to other people."

There was the answer she'd been looking for. "Dr. Batterman... you know Troy then? The sandalwood... Were you—were you one of Troy's clients?" She began to put it all together.

The knife dropped to the floor with a clatter. Raine shut her eyes, turned her head, and exhaled.

The Warden bent down quickly, revealing the balding spot on the top of his head, and picked it back up. He laid it on the table next to her leg.

She felt the cool, flat blade against her thigh; just another reminder of how little physical control she had. But she still had her mind, unlike many of the prisoners above her, who had been there too long and already lost the hope of surviving. She wasn't going to be one of them. She needed to fight, just like she had her whole life.

When he didn't respond to her question, she gathered it must have been true. He had seen her go in and out of the office, and who knew how long he'd been watching her as Troy drilled into his brain.

She tried to change the subject to keep him engaged. "The prison. It's impressive."

The Warden shifted on his feet and scratched the tiny prickles of white hair on his chin.

She thought she saw the hint of a smile, as though he hadn't expected her to flatter him. She suspected this had been the trap Megan fell into as a method of survival. Flatter him. Raine needed to get out of here, and since she was limited in what she could physically do, she was going to have to talk her way out of it. "Why the prison, though?" she asked. "Why the guards?"

"Because I'm doing it better. I've recreated the great experiment. The experiment I wasn't allowed to partake in. It was cut short, but my—*my* experiment will prove human behavior to the world. It will prove that you don't know *what* you would do until you are in the situation. The guards. I don't tell them how to do their job. I don't tell them to beat the prisoners, or throw them in solitary confinement. They act on their own."

She actually did find that interesting. The guards acted how they thought the Warden wanted them to act, to avoid the consequences. So his so called experiment was tainted.

Her thoughts drifted from the guards to the prisoners. These were good people, stolen from their lives. These were not murderers, yet they were treated like criminals. Was this the reason many of them had given up?

Were jails like this in real life? Why did people play the role of their own accord? Because that's what society expected of them? As a psychologist, she was expected to be the levelheaded, sound, anxiety-free one. "You're talking about the prison experiment done at Stanford in the seventies? What do you mean you weren't allowed to take part in it?"

The Warden backed up to the wall, leaned against it, and slid down to the floor.

Raine relaxed a bit as she saw him settle into his thoughts. This could be either good or bad for her. *Keep the conversation moving, just keep it moving. Keep him busy.* She ran those thoughts over and over in her head.

"I was a student at community college back in 1971, when I saw the ad in the paper. $15 a day. That was a lot. I applied. I interviewed. They didn't choose me. Said I showed too many signs of emotional instability."

"So you created your own experiment?" she whispered, looking at him as he pushed his glasses back up the bridge of his nose.

"You're not as stupid as you look."

The words were chilling, but she put up the wall in her mind. She didn't allow his words to penetrate her. "Why did you choose me? Why not take Troy?" She thought she'd try and ask.

He contemplated. Then he stood up quicker than she was expecting, and grabbed the knife from the table. He moved up to her face, just inches away. He used the blade to gently push back a section of her hair, revealing the bloody gash at her hairline. "Because you think you don't deserve this."

She watched him scan her injury, then look down into her eyes. "Nobody deserves this," she said, looking directly back at him, not knowing if that was a mistake.

"Humanity does. All of this, for the cause."

She closed her eyes and tried to stop her lip from quivering, and more tears from pooling. He was going to kill her. He had every intention of killing her when he strapped her to this table. Her last moments on Earth were going to be spent pleading with this madman.

"I've been studying you, studying me." he said in a low voice, chilling her.

"Are you going to kill me?" she asked him. Her voice trembled.

"You'd like that, huh?" he laughed.

She shook her head back and forth. "I don't want to die."

"Interesting… the will. The human desire to survive. It's a shame some of your patients lack that. And you use it to your advantage." He turned from the table and went to the area of the room above her head again.

She couldn't see what he was doing as he fidgeted with tools, clinking them together. She tensed. "If you kill me, then how will you conduct your experiment? You want to observe human behavior, right? How will you do that if you kill your inmates? Do you expect me to be a good little inmate? Everyone responds differently. Take a look at that original experiment in 1971. I studied it too. Did those boys all comply? Did none of them fight back?"

He didn't respond.

She hoped it was because he was contemplating what she said.

He came back around to her side with a syringe, a needle that looked thicker and longer than any she'd ever seen. He poked it into a vial of clear liquid, then tossed the now empty container into the corner of the room.

She squeezed her eyes shut when the vial shattered.

The Warden twisted her forearm to face the ceiling. He slapped it, trying to raise a vein.

"My family will be looking for me," she warned.

"No. No they won't."

She shuddered. *What did he do to them? What did he do to my family?* She instantly thought of the nice guard's family, and his biggest fear.

He set the needle down on the table next to her. The syringe was touching her bare skin. She tensed up. She needed to buy more time.

The Warden moved out of her line of sight and returned with an electronic tablet. He poked the screen for a moment, his face illuminated by the light.

She saw a reflection of flames in his eyes before he turned the image for her to see.

It was a car. Her car. In flames. The red, orange, and black licked the vehicle and twisted in every direction as a camera panned over to a fire safety vehicle arriving at the scene. A reporter hunched over in front of the camera with her microphone, rapidly speaking words that Raine could not hear. But the banner was vivid underneath the clip, "Deadly Car Fire on Outer Road".

He ripped the screen back from her gaze and swiped his finger on the touch pad. He read from an article, "Woman's car crashed in a suburban backwoods outside of the Bay Area. Car fire. Body badly burned. Authorities are looking into dental fragments to identify the body, but the car is registered to a Dr. Raine Walsh, 28, psychologist."

She couldn't believe what she was hearing. But as he spoke the words, the colors of the memory became vivid in her mind. This entire time she had no clue how she'd gotten here. Now it started to become clear once more. It was her facing her trauma, as she had helped so many of her clients before.

"Nobody is looking for you, because they are grieving your death."

FIFTEEN

It was a violent torrential rain. Clutching the wheel. Lights in the rearview mirror. Blinding white lights. Screeching tires on the smeared wet pavement. The grinding of metal. Pain. Red. Flickering red and orange and yellow. And then a man. Help.

The ice sunk into the glass and floated back to the top. Raine added a few more cubes to each before picking up the cocktails and carrying them out of Marcus's kitchen, into the family room.

"Thank you." He took the glass from her, sipped it, and set it on the coffee table.

She leaned over and slid a coaster under it. Habit.

"I don't know what you're so worried about. I'm cool with just doing what we're doing. As long as there are boundaries. I enjoy spending time with you, you know that. Obviously I'm into you. I'd like something more. But, I also understand."

She smoothed her hair up into a ponytail and tied it with the black hair tie from her wrist. "I just... I don't know. I think we complicated things when we slept together," she said quietly, picking her glass back up and taking a big swig of the clear liquid that stung her throat as it went down.

"You didn't enjoy it?" Marcus leaned back in the couch.

"It's not that." She laughed under her breath. "We work together. We have a history. We've been close friends since college."

"Please don't give me the line that you don't want to ruin our friendship. Anything but that."

She tilted her head. "I don't want to hurt you."

"And how would you feel if you saw me with another girl?"

She thought about it, and shook her head. "I'd hate it."

"Hm. So you don't want me, but you don't want anyone else to have me?"

He had a point. She sighed. "Can I just ask that we step back then? No more complications. No gray areas."

"Anything you want. If you want to be just friends, then lets be just friends. If it's what I have to do in order to spend time with you outside of work, then I'm cool with that."

She turned and searched his face. *Was he?*

He was calm and collected, as always.

"But I don't want it to just be what I want." She downed the rest of her drink.

He smiled. "It's not complicated, Raine. I can do the friend thing. It's okay."

She nodded.

He reached for her glass and stood up, walking towards the tiny kitchen. "Is that all you wanted to talk about tonight?" he asked. "I can tell something's wrong.

And I know it's not just our relationship status." He raised an eyebrow at her.

"Yeah... uh, have you talked to Troy at all?"

"Aw shit, is he still giving you trouble?" The glass slipped from his hand into the sink.

Raine adjusted herself on the couch. "He stayed late one night when I did. I didn't know he was still in the office."

Marcus leaned against the kitchen sink and crossed his arms over his chest. "What did he do?" His voice was low.

"Well he—he manipulated me into giving him a private a yoga class."

"Seriously?"

"Well it didn't last long. I caught him staring and he made an inappropriate comment about my ass."

Marcus threw his hands in the air. "All right, that's it." He reached for his phone on the end table.

Raine stood and held her hands out in front of her. "Hey it's okay. I don't want to upset you. It was just uncomfortable and I told Melita about it, she thought I should tell you."

"Yeah, no. Raine." He stepped into her arms.

She wrapped them around him, embracing him.

"I'm upset because you had to go through that. I don't want you to think... well I mean I've made comments about your ass before. I'll stop. I'm sorry."

She backed up. "There's a difference, Marcus. It's okay for you to say something like that because I let you. It's consent. I did not give Troy my permission and he knows it."

Marcus nodded. "We're going to do something about this, okay? How about we all sit down and have a conference. We can invite Sylvie to take notes. Lets try to talk this out, and if nothing changes after that, we call the authorities and get the hell out."

Raine nodded. "Okay." She watched Marcus cross over to the window. "I should probably get going."

"You realize there's a storm passing through right now? It's really coming down out there. Maybe you should wait." He peered around the curtains to the darkness outside.

"Naw, I'll be fine." She smoothed out the fabric of her magenta shirt.

"You know I have room here for you to sleep. You take the bed. I'll sleep on the couch."

That was almost enough to convince her. It was late. It was storming. The safer choice would be to just stay the night and leave in the morning. "I don't want Viona to be by herself tonight. She hates thunderstorms. I've driven in storms before, I'll be okay." This was the truth. If she hadn't lived alone, if she'd had a roommate to let her dog out when she couldn't make it back home because of a terrible storm, she wouldn't have to worry. "I'll see you later." She turned to grab her purse, and looked over her shoulder to smile at him.

He rounded the couch and walked with her to the door of his apartment, opening it and holding it for her. "Drive safe, okay? Text me when you make it home."

"Will do." Normally, they would kiss, but this time she felt weird about it. She just patted his chest with her hand and turned to leave. "Have a good night, Marcus." She smiled at him and headed down the hall to the stairs.

Outside, Raine tucked her chin to her chest and burst out from under the awning. She'd already hit the button on her key fob. Her car headlights blinked twice and she reached out for the door handle, whipped open the driver's side door, and thrust herself into the seat. She shut the door behind her and breathed out into the car, allowing her whole body to shiver. She locked the doors, dropped her purse on the passenger seat, and shoved the key into the ignition. The engine revved.

It was just rain, cold drops that plummeted down like needles on the pavement and smeared her windshield. She sat in Marcus's apartment parking lot, getting her bearings and waiting for the defroster to kick on. She didn't catch the news that there'd be a big storm passing through the area. She looked at the radio clock. It was a little past 11:30, almost midnight. The only thing she had on her side was that hopefully other people were smarter than her and would stay home. It was to her advantage that not many other people should be on the road.

She reached into her purse, pulled out her cell phone, and dropped it on the driver's seat between her legs. It was her safety blanket. She used the thing for directions, to call for help if she had car troubles, etc. She'd become more and more dependent on it. But with a night like tonight, she liked to know that she wasn't alone; that there was help just on the other side of that device if she needed it.

The defroster melted away the fog on the windshield enough for her to make an attempt at getting on the road. Her apartment in Noe Valley was a little less than a thirty-minute drive. She never understood why

Marcus liked to be so far out of the city. He must have liked the idea of suburbia.

She pulled her seatbelt across her chest and clicked it into the buckle, then eased out onto the street. She set off down the road, squinting through the fog. It felt better to lean against the steering wheel, her muscles tense, and she pushed through water on the pitch black, waterlogged road. The wind pushed her back and forth, the pellets of rain smacking into her windshield. It was almost hard to not stare off into the raindrops. The rain in her headlights looked something like a spaceship going into hyperspace in Star Wars.

As she rounded a corner, her front wheels dropped into a pothole and she hydroplaned. Her stomach flipped, like on the downhill of a roller coaster, as she straightened her spine.

You're not invincible. It was enough to snap her back to attention, squinting between the droplets. The windshield wipers beat against the glass like the sound of her heart.

Luckily, as expected, there weren't many cars on the road. The fewer cars there were, the easier it was to see the white lines on the road. She blinked each time a lightning bolt shattered the sky on the horizon in front of her. The two lane road wound through trees on both sides, just one lane for her and one for oncoming traffic.

She checked her rearview mirror. There were headlights on the road behind her. She sped up to try and distance herself from the car, to keep from being blinded by its high beams.

She sped up, but she was no match for the car behind her. They tailgated her, the lights so bright she couldn't even tell what the vehicle looked like.

"Get off my ass!" she yelled out into the car. Her eyes moved from the road in front of her to the rearview mirror and back again.

She reached forward and flipped her hazard lights on.

Hopefully that'll get them to go around me, she thought as she approached a wide turn in the road.

It didn't.

The car swerved over to the oncoming traffic lane, then moved back into the lane behind her.

She gasped, instinctively jerked her car away from them and slammed on the brakes. The cell phone between her legs went flying to the floor in front of her and settled at the pedals by her feet.

"What in the world!" she yelled, angry as she tried to locate her phone safety blanket.

Panic set in. It was clear the car was trying to run her off the road. She moved over to the left lane and desperately hoped that no oncoming traffic emerged around the next bend. The other car duplicated her move, refusing to pass.

They were definitely following her. Her breath quickened.

She couldn't reach her phone.

She eased back into the correct lane and pressed her foot down on the pedal as far as she could. The car accelerated, pushing her back into her seat. She was almost panting, whimpering in terror.

The lights continued to blind her, and before she could react, the road opened up to an intersection. She broke away from the car behind her, blew the glowing red octagonal stop sign, and sent her car into a spin.

Her vehicle rotated several times and stopped. The lights bore down on her.

There was an ear-wrenching screech.

She gripped the steering wheel as she saw the shadow of a dark figure inside the vehicle in front of her. The events proceeded in slow motion.

Grinding metal.

Smash.

Her neck snapped forward.

Red.

Black.

Heartbeat.

Buh bum. Buh bum. Buh bum.

A faint ringing sound pierced her semi consciousness.

She moved her left arm, the only thing she could move, up to the pain in her face. Crimson wet liquid smeared her hand.

Her thoughts were jumbled. Fearful.

Through the shattered glass of her windshield, the dark figure appeared again. It rounded the car and yanked open her door.

She tried to call out to them. "Help-" Her voice was hoarse and low, her throat burned.

The pain of a thousand needles pierced her body as her seatbelt was cut away and she was yanked from the car.

Her consciousness was fading now. Lying down on the wet pavement. The figure stood and moved to the twisted metal. They fumbled with something. A bright orange-red light burst in front of her, and suddenly her aching, shivering body was warm.

The figure loomed over her.

There was a sharp prick in her arm, more defined than the cocoon of pain she was enveloped in. And then the sleep came, and robbed her of her broken consciousness.

SIXTEEN

Raine squirmed in her restraints. The straps on her wrists tightened. She resisted, the ache of her memories surging through her.

The Warden grazed her hipbone with the back of his hand as his fingers closed around the syringe once more. She pressed her chin into her neck, trying to see her forearm. The crook of her elbow was black and blue, bruised from all the times she'd been pricked.

How long have I even been here since the crash? she thought, her perception of time or even time of day was completely shot. She watched the Warden as his thick, large framed glasses slid down the bridge of his nose again. He squinted as he shoved the glasses back up with one hand, and looked down at her forearm. He tapped her arm again, trying to raise a vein.

He's having trouble.

He reached into his pocket and grabbed out a strap of the same material her restraints were made out of. She concluded this strap was probably for her mouth, though he didn't feel the need to use it. He slid the strap underneath her bicep and tied a knot, pulling it tight around her arm. Too tight.

Raine winced as he squeezed. The circulation cut off, a tingle replaced the flow of energy. The blue lines in her arm swelled.

"Please," she pleaded, trying to catch his eye. "Please can I be awake for this? Don't put me to sleep again."

He ran his calloused hand up her arm.

"I'm sick of falling asleep and not knowing what's happened." She held her breath and squeezed her eyes shut as the Warden pierced the skin of her arm with the needle.

He held it there a moment, the needle wobbled in her sore skin before he slid it back out and dropped it on the table.

She was still conscious. She opened her eyes; he had turned away. The syringe lay by her side once more, liquid still intact.

Should I say thank you? Her mind raced.

Without turning back around, he walked away from her table and slammed the door behind him.

SEVENTEEN

Her family thought she was dead. There were news clips and articles written about it. Did that just happen? Had it been weeks? She had been so close to escaping this hellhole, before she wandered right into the spider's web. And he'd tried to use his venom to impair her again. But he didn't. She didn't know whether this was a good thing or a bad thing.

Time was nonexistent in that small, white room. Mere minutes could have passed, or it could have been hours that she lay on that table. She moved herself into a meditative state, trying to block out all other stimuli. Her aching body. The vulnerability of exposure. The lack of control.

The arm where the needle entered was crusted with a trickle of dried blood. As she lay in her meditative state, the door creaked open. She startled, and stared straight up at the ceiling. She anticipated the worst.

"My god… " The soft voice dripped with empathy.

She turned her head. It was the night guard that confided in her. The nice guard that had without a doubt, purposely left her cage unlocked.

She watched him approach her, reach above and grab a tool from a tray above her head.

He looked her in the eyes, his face flushed. "Are you hurt?" he asked.

Her eyes welled up. *I don't know.* "I'm okay," she croaked, "What's going on? Were you the one that unlo-"

"I was instructed to escort you back to your cell." The tone of his voice changed as he cut her off. It sounded authoritative.

He's watching, Raine gathered.

The Warden orchestrated everything. This was all a big experiment of human nature to him. She was a lab rat. The guard in front of her was also a lab rat.

Her arms were limp as he used the tool to unlatch the restraints from the hooks on the wall. He undid the strap at her wrist. Her arm flopped off the table. She had no control over it. The surging pain wrestled through her muscles, the effects of staying in the same position for so long.

He lifted her arm and put it back on the table, so that it wasn't dangling.

She pulled her achy arms in, one by one, and covered her breasts.

The guard looked away a moment, then turned to work on her ankle restraints.

She saw his look of disgust as he worked to set her free of the bonds. She noticed how he avoided looking at her. His hatred at the situation and for his captor radiated through his fingers as he cut the leather restraint.

"Can you stand?" he asked.

She moved her legs. They were wobbly, like a baby giraffe learning to walk. She lifted her head too quickly, the room spun, and she swayed back down.

He reached forward and caught the small of her back, helping her put one foot on the floor at a time and hoisted her up.

"Do you have clothes?"

"If you cooperate, I won't have to put you in cuffs when we head back upstairs." As he spoke, his eyes searched the room.

She nodded her head in compliance. *I'll cooperate.*

He guided her through the door.

She looked over her shoulder at the table that the Warden must have set up in the room after she'd been knocked out. There was a medical tray on wheels directly above the top of the table, with all kinds of tools. She exhaled a shaky breath as she eyed all the different contraptions. It could have been much worse for her on that table. *For some reason, he must like me. Or I wouldn't still be alive. I'm one of the only ones that's seen who he is, and he didn't kill me... yet.* She was hopeful that her words, her experience as a psychologist, and speaking to those with mental instabilities had paid off.

As they exited the room, she looked straight ahead. The loft was gone.

It wasn't gone entirely, but down the hallway, there was a galvanized metal steel door blocking the hall from the rest of the loft. *This guard doesn't even know there's a living space on the other side of this wall! It's all jail for him!* She couldn't believe her eyes at the transformation that had been wrought and what it covered up. To the guard, who was assigned to come down and retrieve her, this was just another level of rooms.

As they crossed over the threshold, Raine in front of the guard, she tripped over something squishy. They both looked down to find her gown. She looked over her shoulder and the guard nodded. She bent down and picked it up. It was the same gown as before, bloodied, dirty, and stained. She slipped it over her head and it dropped over her aching body. To have some sort of privacy again was a privilege, and she was happy to have it, even though it wasn't the most ideal.

The guard guided her through the door on their right, the door that she thought was a bathroom before.

It wasn't a bathroom. It was another staircase. She couldn't understand the logistics of this building, except that it had been engineered and designed for the Warden's little game. Nooks and crannies everywhere. Different vacant rooms for different purposes. Staircases that only led up from this floor. The area where he himself lived, that was apparently hidden from the rest.

She didn't understand it.

She continued to walk in front of the guard, one step at a time up the stairs and into the familiar hallway outside the warehouse. She kept her eyes peeled for signs of cameras, something she'd looked for before, but hadn't seen. If the Warden wasn't watching her before, she was sure he was watching now. The Warden had been one of Troy's clients. The problem was, he could have been treated by Troy at any time in the history of their practice. It might or might not even be one of his current clients. Either way, she'd never be able to identify him, because all of their client information was kept locked up and private. There might not even be any records that indicated this guy had ever visited their office, if it was far enough in the past. And all sessions with their clients were kept confidential, unless of course the patient was a danger to themselves or others. Troy missed the bus on this one.

Unless… was it possible he still could have something to do with this? The way he'd been treating her. The fact that in the last week or so he'd been busy and kept to himself. There was that one late night in the office. The scratches on his arms. The human scratches.

She shook her head to clear those thoughts as they rounded on the double doors to the warehouse. It was crazy. Did she hate Troy *that* much? So much that she'd just met her captor, the psychopath who turned the penthouse of a building into a prison, after he'd kidnapped people from their daily lives and kept actual humans locked up for some twisted experiment he needed to prove to humanity about their behavior. She'd just met this person, yet she still continued to contemplate whether or not Troy could have had something to do with this.

"Hey, night shift."

Raine turned her head to see the guard with the sickly green eyes, the one with authority, poking his head out of a door behind them.

"I'm on assignment, Buck," he grunted back, as he reached forward and gently grabbed her wrist.

The mean guard, who she could now refer to as Buck, with his head shaved bald, had walked out of the room and into the hall. He eyed Raine. "Was she with *him*?" he asked, nodding at her.

"I can't talk right now."

"You could bring her in here before you take her back." He laughed nastily.

Raine straightened her shoulders, her brow furrowed. Her insides flamed up.

"I said I'm on assignment, asshole. I'll be in later." He turned Raine back around, away from the guard, and held her arm while fishing around his pocket and pulling out a set of keys. "All right. Handcuffs for the sake of the other prisoners." He whispered into her ear.

His face grazed hers and she felt his breath on her ear. He secured her hands behind her back. Even though he'd shown her kindness, and confided in her, he was still playing his part. She was grateful for the feeling that he was on her side, but in the end, he was really only on his own side. Part of her felt she should be angry about that, but he needed to be on his own side for his wife. For his daughter.

The metal cuffs were cold against her wrists.

He clasped them together, squeezing them shut. Even though he didn't tighten them completely up to her wrists, just the metal of the handcuffs resting on her skin was painful. Her wrists had just been bound for several hours at least, and her wrists felt raw and sore. She hung her head as he opened the creaking door to the warehouse.

There had to be a little bit of irony in the fact that this guard had left her cage unlocked to assist her in an escape, and he was assigned to take her back. She couldn't help but think that the Warden knew about all of this, and he was messing further with their minds, to see how they'd react.

The musty room before her was depressingly familiar. And even though it was the last place on Earth she wanted to be, it was better than being at the mercy of the Warden, or any of the other guards for that matter.

The guard walked behind her, holding onto her handcuffed hands and guiding her down the row of cages. She looked back and forth, her eyes darting from person to person. There seemed to be fewer people in the cages.

Her heart pounded in her chest as they approached Arie's cage, and hers next to that. Before they arrived, she saw both of Arie's hands curled around the bars.

When she finally made eye contact, she saw the hope drain from his face. She shook her head back and forth, defeated.

She'd failed him. She failed Arie.

He dropped back into the shadows of his cage. The guard continued to guide her. She felt resistance against her wrists as she turned to her cage, and he kept them walking straight.

"I'm not going back in my cage?"

"I'm just following orders," he said quietly.

They turned the corner, and he stopped her in front of a door that had a mail slot in it set at eye level. He let go of her cuffed wrists and unlocked the door.

She peered inside. It was a cell, completely enclosed by solid walls. Though still small, she could stand up in it. It had a twin mattress against one wall, and a toilet in the other corner. There was even a small showerhead next to the toilet, with a drain underneath. No curtain. No shower walls.

She longed for a shower. It'd been so long since she'd had a proper shower, apart from when she was blasted with jets when she arrived here. Though there were luxuries inside this cell, it was completely isolated from anyone else, aside from the small slot in the door that she could look through.

Her thoughts were interrupted by the release of her wrists from the cuffs. Her arms dropped to her sides.

The guard motioned for her to go inside.

"Is this... am I getting special treatment?" she asked, the uneasiness evident in her words.

"I'm sorry." The guard looked into the corner of the cage.

She followed his eyes. A conspicuous camera mounted in the corner.

He looked at the floor as he pulled the gate closed and turned his key in the lock, she heard the click of metal as the latch caught.

EIGHTEEN

Raine sat on the cold, concrete floor of her cell. Her toes were close to the drain, and she sat with her knees up to her chest. She rested her head on her knees and allowed the frigid water to flow over the back of her neck and bare bottom. Her hair was flipped over, laying in strands down her legs. When her chestnut hair was wet, it appeared almost jet black. The cold water washed away the filth of her time there and swirled down the drain. She'd looked up at the camera once, a constant reminder that she was being watched. And a little more closely now since her attempted escape. Though she still couldn't understand why the Warden was granting her privileges. She also wasn't sure if she *was* getting privileges, or if the worst was yet to come.

Even though the water was freezing, it was comforting beating on her back. When her fingers and toes became wrinkly, she reached up and squeaked the faucet off. She sat there and twisted her hair, wringing out the water. She used her gown to dry off her body, slipped it over her head, and made her way to the bed. There were worse things than a damp gown, and by the time it dried, she'd probably be ready for another shower.

The days had run together, and her vision of reality became a blur. She was a prisoner. She lived the life of a prisoner now.

She called out on several occasions to see if any other prisoners could hear her, but there was no response. One of the nasty dayshift guards told her she'd been re-moved from the others because she was disturbing to them. She'd behave better if she were alone.

As she dozed the alarm blared, though it didn't surprise her this time, because they were frequent oc-currences.

What she couldn't get used to was what happened when these alarms went off. Somebody was always re-trieved from the cages. And nobody ever knew what hap-pened to them when they were taken. Most of the time they'd come back unconscious, or injured, like the time Arie was taken.

She stayed seated on her bed, until she heard cages begin to rattle.

She leaped up and scurried over to the slit in the door. Her eyes darted both ways. There was lots of shout-ing and talking, and when she saw the guards rounding the corner with a line of inmates, she gasped. She flat-tened her palms against the metal and pressed her fore-head against the door.

One by one the inmates walked around the bend, tied to one another. She searched their faces.

Arie.

"Hey!" she shouted. The inmates didn't look, ex-cept the tall, lanky, boy with blackened eyes. He stole a glance at her cell.

She reached up and touched her wet hair. She was allowed to shower. She was allowed to stand, for that matter. How would the other inmates see her? Would Arie think she'd given herself to the Warden?

She thought she saw a hint of a nod in her direction from Arie before a guard blocked her view, shepherding the line of prisoners.

"Hey, you! Do I get to go too?" she blurted out.

The guard remained with his back to her. When the last inmate rounded the corner, he walked away.

"Hey!"

"Shut your mouth," he snarled over his shoulder, and slammed the heavy doors behind him.

Where are they taking them? She panicked.

She'd never felt more alone.

NINETEEN

Time was completely distorted inside the concrete walls. She lay on the bed, her head hanging off it, and her hair swayed underneath. Her hair had dried, which told her it had at least been that long since the guards took the rest of the inmates away from the warehouse. She allowed the blood to rush to her head, her temples beating, before she pulled herself up. Her stomach grumbled under her gown, and she tried to massage away the hunger.

The door to the warehouse creaked open, just a crack. Raine leaped up, standing at attention.

They're back, she thought. Her mind raced. She hurried back to the slot. Just when she thought nobody was coming, a pale petite girl with long, dusty orange hair emerged from the door. She turned and made eye contact.

Raine remained quiet. She didn't know what to say.

The girl wore a shirt and pants, the same material as the gown, that reminded her of scrubs. She was carrying a glass and bowl in her hands. She had to set them on the floor to turn and close the heavy door. She knelt down, picked them back up, and walked towards the solitary confinement cell.

Raine eyed the cup and bowl, her stomach grumbling. She regretted the sight. *How is she going to get those in here?* She backed up, her eyes wide as the girl unlocked the door.

"Are you- what's happening?" she asked. *Is she helping me, or… ?*

The girl stepped into the cage and locked herself inside, then tossed the keys through the slot, as far away as she could launch them.

"Why'd you… why'd you do that? What the hell!" Anger filled up the emotional void she'd been living in. Those keys were her ticket to getting out of this cell, and quite possibly out of the building. She wasn't afraid of trying to escape another time, despite what happened the last time. If she didn't fight, there was no reason to exist. She'd either escape, or die trying.

"Where did you get those keys?" Raine's voice was frantic.

The orange-haired, freckled girl looked up at the camera, and back at her. "Where do you *think* I got those keys?" she asked. Her voice was soft and kind, almost like a squeak from a tiny mouse.

Raine spun on her heels and made her way back to the bed, plopping down on it. She did not expect that.

Then it hit her. It was obvious now. Arie had never described what she looked like. But the way this girl carried herself. The way she had access. "You're Meg," she whispered.

The girl's lips tugged up into a small smile. She nodded.

How do I know I can trust this girl? The Warden gave her keys? He trusted her with them. How do I know she's not helping him, or part of this whole experiment to begin with?

Megan sat next to her, their thighs touching. "I know you haven't eaten in a while. It's not much... "

"Thank you," she breathed. She took the bowl of oatmeal, and water glass. She brought the glass to her lips, and started gulping.

"Whoa, slow down. You're going to need that to wash down this mush." She smiled.

Raine stifled a laugh. She was right. The cereal she'd been fed since she arrived here was tasteless, oatmeal-textured mush. Megan handed her the bowl, and Raine used her fingers to spoon it up into her mouth. Mush, regardless, this was warm mush. She hadn't eaten anything warm since she'd gotten there, and her belly welcomed it. She hardly chewed it before she swallowed, and washed it down with the water.

She felt Megan's eyes on her. When she finished eating, she set the cup and bowl on the floor, and turned to look at the girl.

She was pretty, dainty and comforting. "He likes you," she said softly, and brushed a strand of Raine's hair off her forehead.

Her muscles tightened.

"If he didn't, you wouldn't still be here."

"Maybe that would be better."

Because of her practice with yoga and meditation, as well as studying the minds of humans, she had a great perception of people's energies. Megan had soothing energy. She wasn't threatening.

Just talking to someone was a relief after the amount of time she'd spent in that cell. And the first time she'd seen any people apart from guards was when they were taking them all away. She began to cry, the tears falling helplessly from her eyes.

"Shhh." Megan soothed her. She guided Raine's head to her lap, and stroked her hair.

Raine cried into Megan's knees, and loved the feeling of gentle fingers through her hair. "Meg, he said you were the only other one that's seen him?"

"Did he hurt you? Did he rape you?"

"No," she breathed. "Did he hurt you?"

Meg didn't say anything. The silence was answer enough.

Raine felt overwhelmed again at how lucky she'd been. And the circumstances all made sense to her. She wasn't getting special treatment. Megan was the one that got to wear pants. She was trusted to walk around the prison. He'd even entrusted her with keys. He had psychologically manipulated this young woman, to the point where she was able to have more freedom than the others, but it all came at a cost.

"I'm the first person he ever took. It was two years yesterday."

"I'm so sorry, Meg." She *was* sorry. But just hearing that sucked the hope right out of her. Two years. Could she, herself, last two years in this place? Why had it been so long? Had she attempted to escape? Something kept her here, whether it was her own will, or whether it was the external factor that was the nucleus of all their problems.

The girl continued to run her fingers through Raine's hair. "I don't remember life outside of here. And, I don't think I want to go back."

Raine sat up and wiped her eyes with the backs of her hands. "Are you crazy?" she whispered, glancing at the camera and back again.

"If I went back, everything would be different. I just can't face that."

She grabbed Megan's shoulder and whispered into her ear, "Aren't you tired of being a prisoner? That man stole your life."

Megan shook her head.

"How do I know I can trust you?" Raine asked, narrowing her eyes. She didn't know this girl. She could have been sent in here by the Warden to figure out Raine's state of mind, to see if she'd be more to his liking.

"Arie and I are so close because we made a connection when he was first brought here. I was the one that calmed him down. When he woke up from the anesthesia, he was thrashing around like a dog with rabies in a cage," Megan said.

The comparison was almost comical, considering the profession Arie came from. Raine wasn't sure that Megan made the connection, unless she was just messing with her.

She continued, "I say I don't want to go back because I can't have a life out there anymore, but with Arie... he's a light in this dark place. He reminds me every day that maybe it *is* possible. His enthusiasm, after being beaten down so many times by the guards, is inspiring. I understand why you're drawn to him."

Raine felt bad. Guilt flooded her. "I… " *Drawn to him?* Come to think of it, she *had* felt a connection with Arie, of course. He was the first thing that made sense in this place. She shared private, past experiences with him that she hadn't even told Marcus. *Marcus…* If Megan was bringing up Arie now, she must know what they shared next to each other in the cages. "Well, Arie is truly something. But I have a boyfriend." The taste of the word felt unnatural on her tongue, but it comforted her to think that Marcus had always and would always be there for her no matter what.

"Had. If your boyfriend thinks you're dead, he's probably moved on."

The world came crashing down on her again. *Marcus thinks I'm dead.* She bawled once more, wiping at her eyes and sniffling.

After a moment of mourning the loss of her own life, Raine collected herself and brought her attention back to the situation at hand. "Where did the guards take everybody?" she asked.

"The yard," Megan whispered.

"What's that?" She vaguely remembered Arie telling her about the yard.

"Inmates are allowed to go out to the yard when the weather permits. You're under strict lockdown because of what happened, so you had to stay here. But the yard is the roof of the prison."

She soaked in this bit of information. "He takes everyone to the roof? To get some fresh air and sun?"

"Well, sort of. By weather permitting, I mean, we're only allowed to go to the yard when it's foggy outside. We can't see anything past our hand. But it's nice to breathe in outside air. It's cleansing really. But most of the time, it's so disorienting, you can't even tell where you are. It's like we're in the sky."

Raine listened to Megan's soft voice. She seemed like such a fragile, gentle person. *How has she survived in this place so long?* The thought brought her mind back to some of the many clients she'd been able to talk to about their stresses in life. She remembered specifically telling a teenage girl, an introvert who had been through some trauma at her high school, that a reed could survive a storm easier than a tree. Megan had many of the same characteristics as that teenage girl. It didn't matter what the world saw on the outside. *Strength comes from within.*

The door to the warehouse opened again. She stood up and squinted at the mailbox sized slot to see if everyone was coming back, she hoped to catch a glance of Arie's face once more.

But the body that rounded the door was not a guard. It was not an inmate.

His slouched shoulders stopped in the dim light that poured through the doorway, casting a long shadow up to the solid door of her cell.

It was as if Megan could tell who it was from the sound of his footstep. "He didn't like me talking about the yard." Megan whispered to Raine, grabbing her hand and squeezing. "Our time here is done." She stood up.

"Please stay with me," Raine pleaded. She enjoyed Megan's company. Her energy was calming. But she already knew the answer. She looked over at him, a glare reflecting off his glasses so it was impossible to see his intentions. He knelt down and picked up the keys Megan had thrown earlier. With the keys jingling at each step, he slowly approached the cell. He had a hint of a smile on his lips.

She felt Megan tense up next to her as she stood. Then the girl walked forward.

The Warden unlocked the door, grabbed Megan by the hair, and pulled her out of the cell. He slammed the door behind her, locking Raine back in. Then, in front of the door, he pulled Megan towards him.

Raine trembled as she watched through the slot, as their lips touched. She saw Megan's hand behind her back, balling up into a fist as the Warden kissed her.

Raine felt bile rise in her throat. She was frustrated. She was angry. She couldn't stand watching this man take advantage of them whenever he wanted. And she didn't understand the dynamic of Megan and the Warden. Megan was his slave, but she gave in to it. Was that the only way she was able to survive here?

And what was going to happen to Raine?

The Warden never spoke. When he was done fondling Megan in front of her, the two of them walked out of the warehouse together, and the door slammed behind them.

But before Megan's glowing, orange hair left the warehouse, she looked back at Raine in the cell and gave a small nod. The nod was enough to tell Raine that their conversation wasn't over. That she would be back for more when she got the chance.

That they were on the same side.

TWENTY

Sometime while she was sleeping, the guards brought all the inmates back into their cages. While she couldn't see anybody else, and their cages were away from her cell, she could still hear faint cries and people talking to one another every now and then.

She heard some shouting, and a guard turned the corner and approached on her cell, keys out.

She rose from her seat. She had never dealt with this guard before. He was a day shift. His evil counterpart, Buck, must have been off busy somewhere. He marched up to her cage and looked through the slot at her.

She stepped back.

"No funny business. I unlock this, you get cuffed. You walk with me to your relocation. End of story, got it?"

"My relocation?" she asked.

"And no questions," he finished.

She nodded, turned around, and put her hands at the small of her back.

He did as he said he would—opened the door, and clipped the cuffs around her wrists. He pulled her out.

She tiptoed back and then forward again as he guided her down the row of cages.

He walked her back to the cage she'd initially been in before. The cage next to Arie's. She saw him come back to the front of his cage.

The guard unlocked the cuffs. "On your knees."

She hesitated, and then dropped to her knees, a little too hard. Her kneecaps banged against the concrete and she winced. As she crawled into the cage, the door slammed shut and locked behind her. The guard walked off and out of sight before she even had time to turn around.

"Welcome back, neighbor." Arie called out to her.

She smiled as memories of her whereabouts away from this cage flooded back to her. "I tried, Arie. I'm so sorry." She pushed her hands out of the bars, next to his wall. There was hesitation, but then his fingers brushed hers.

"I'm not upset. You tried your best," he said, his voice just barely above an inaudible whisper.

"Why did they move me back here?" she asked, not sure he knew the answer, though he had been here longer than her. He knew the alarm sounds and what they meant, and their frequency.

"Make room for a new prisoner," he answered. Something in her heart pricked. "Are you serious? That fast, huh?"

"It's different every time. This is good for you, though. Means the attention won't be on you as much. Look, he's already moved you out of lockdown and back here. That has to mean something."

"I thought you guys would hate me and think I was getting special treatment. I thought you'd think I gave it up to him, like... well, you know."

"Like Meg," he finished. There was silence between them. Arie's words were hurt.

"She's doing what she has to, to survive."

"Did you?"

"What?"

"Did you give it up to him?"

Raine pulled her fingers back.

"I'm sorry." He seemed to be pressing his face against the bars, as his speech was a little impaired. "You did what you had to do-"

"Hello. No. I didn't give it up to him, Arie," she responded. "Though I'm not sure how much of a choice I'll have if he gets me in his hands again. It was awful."

"You don't have to tell me." Arie croaked.

She didn't. "Enough about me. How was the yard?" she asked.

"How did you know?"

"I spent some time with Megan when everyone was gone. She came to me."

He was quiet. "She used to come to me."

"Maybe she goes to those that need it most, Arie. Maybe she doesn't think you need her encouragement right now?"

"Encouragement? Is that what you got from her?" he asked.

He was right. She hadn't necessarily given Raine hope during their visit. If anything, she hinted that she shouldn't try and escape again or things would get even worse for her. She told Raine that she'd been there for two years, and pretty much any attempt she'd made to get back to her normal life was shot.

"The yard was fine. I never quite understand it. It's disorienting. We're given something by the guards."

"Given something?"

"A capsule. A pill to take, in little paper cups. We stand in line, they administer it. If we don't swallow and show our open mouth and tongues, then we can't go outside."

"You think he gives you drugs to confuse you as to where you are?"

"Yes. That's exactly what it is. But the breath of fresh air is worth it. But even though I'm aware of what's going on, everything is quite disorienting. It's a muted brightness. Cloudy. Foggy. That's all I know."

"How did you know a new prisoner was being put into that cell after me?" she asked.

"I heard two of the guards talking about how they had a new one at receiving and he was fighting them. It was only a matter of time before they went straight to solitary confinement."

She leaned back in the cage and listened.

Arie continued, "We'll see soon enough who the next victim is. The only problem is, whenever somebody new comes, he always gets rid of one."

"Like, kills them?" she asked, her voice shaky.

"We don't know what happens to them. Someone always disappears from the cages."

Her mind worked furiously at the possibilities of the new situation.

"Do we have another plan?" she asked, hesitant.

"Me? I always have a plan."

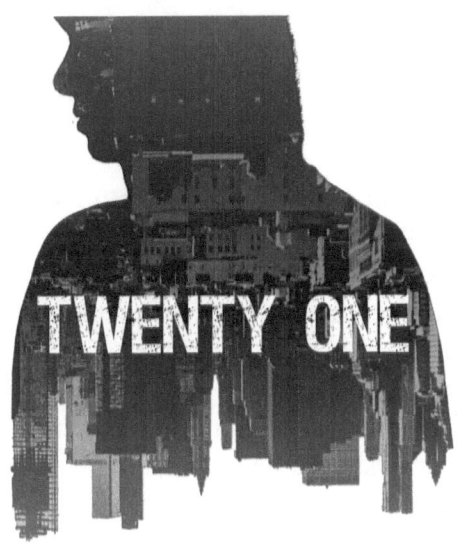

TWENTY ONE

She'd forgotten how cramped these cages were. Her legs were beginning to fall asleep, and she tried a few different seated poses to stretch them out and try to bring circulation back to them. She reached up and touched the tender area above her cheekbones, the pressure in her head pounding. The area around her eyes was sensitive, and for once she couldn't wait for the guards to shut off the lights and make the prison pitch black. Usually that was a time of anxiety for her, but this time she welcomed it.

It wasn't long after, her wish was granted. The lights went out and her eyes adjusted to the dim light.

"G'night Arie," she mumbled, and placed her hand on the wall between them.

"Goodnight Raine," he reciprocated, "I uh, I can't stop thinking about you," he said.

She opened her eyes. She wasn't expecting that.

"I'm sorry. I just thought you should know."

She sighed, her muscles relaxing. "No, same," she whispered. Her eyes fluttered closed once more, for just a moment, when the door to the warehouse screeched open. A guard she didn't recognize burst through the door, flashlight in hand. Since it wasn't Buck, and it wasn't the guard that returned her to her cage, they must have switched to the night shift.

He didn't bother to turn on the overhead lights, but many of the others in their cages stirred in the beam of the flashlight.

Raine ignored the commotion and tried to close her eyes again when she heard her own cage rattle. She opened her eyes to see the shadow in front of her door. "What's going on?" she asked.

He rattled the keys in her door, "Let's go. He wants to see you."

Her heart raced. "No," she said firmly.

The guard turned his head. "Don't make this diffi-cult." He narrowed his eyes and patted the side of his belt where the baton was stashed.

She turned and crawled out on her hands and knees.

Without bothering to cuff her again, he grabbed her arm.

She winced as his hand pinched the sensitive area under her arm, and she left the warehouse with him.

It all happened so fast. She had no clue where they were headed. "What did I do? Why does the Warden want to see me?" she pleaded.

He choked on what she thought was a laugh. "The Warden? Naw, that's not who I'm talking about."

They stopped outside of the door to one of the holding rooms.

"Who then?" she asked. Her brow furrowed.

"He's been asking for you ever since he was brought in. Asking for you through his entire intake. He won't shut up about it."

He unlocked the door, grabbed her by the back of the neck and threw her into the small room. The door closed and the sickening scrape of the lock clicked.

TWENTY TWO

She choked in the guard's grasp as she was tossed into the room. She rubbed her neck, leaned forward, and clutched at the doorknob.

Locked. The room was small; the size of a walk-in closet, even smaller than the room with the bed and camera.

He sat restrained to a wooden chair in the middle of the room. Leather straps bound his arms and legs.

"Troy?" she heaved.

His face was close to unrecognizable. His eyes were bruised blue and purple, and his lip was swollen. He had a huge gash on his upper cheekbone.

"Raine," he lisped.

"How the hell did you end up here?" she asked. She didn't move. She couldn't believe her eyes. She couldn't believe that even though he was the one in restraints, she still didn't trust him.

"Look at you. You're alive." He took his time, and his words were slurred. His bloody teeth poked out from under his lip.

She nodded. She crossed her arms over her chest and bit her lip to keep from showing emotion on her face.

"Ever since you were taken, I was blamed for it. Especially by Marcus."

"How'd you know I was taken? The Warden told me you all thought I was dead."

"We did. But then I looked into it. Sure, your car was found burned up. But they would never answer questions about your body. The evidence has been impounded, obviously. They won't tell the public anything. I think—I think the conspiracy is that law enforcement is embarrassed they couldn't straight-out say they didn't find a body. Who would suspect that a monster would replace your body... with another?" he coughed, hacking over his chest. He wore a gown identical to hers, though his was stained with fresh blood. "I think I'm here because I was close to solving the case. And look at that-I found youuu." He grinned. There was something chilling about the way he sung the words.

A pang of intuition told her something was seriously wrong. The constant harassment and threats he made to her when they worked together. The sandalwood. The scratches on his arm that night. The fact that there was a possibility he knew she'd be leaving late from Marcus'. Troy was one of the only ones who knew they'd been seeing each other, apart from her friend Melita of course.

And there was the fact that she still couldn't clearly see the face of the shadowy image in her memory of the car wreck.

She crossed her arms over her chest. "Cut the shit, Troy."

He laughed airily, the swollen lip not impairing his smirk. He looked up at her with narrowed eyes. "I've been beaten and strung up to a chair. My dick has been sprayed down by a water blaster, and you think there's a possibility I might have something to do with this whole charade? I may call out a nice piece of ass when I see one, but I ain't this twisted." His head dropped, as if to recover from the energy it took to impart that message to her.

She let her arms fall to her sides. "The Warden said he was one of your patients. Who is he?" she asked.

"The Warden?"

"The man responsible for all this. Now who is he?"

"I've been here a total of one night. You're telling me you don't even know who kidnapped you?"

"Do you?"

Silence.

He squirmed in the chair. "He was my client. A while back he stopped coming for sessions. Disappeared. He'd talk about… " He stopped to catch his breath, tried to lean forward and then lifted his head again. "He'd talk about psychological experiment archives. He was particularly fond of the professor who conducted the prison experiment. He talked a lot in our sessions about how he could do it better."

She contemplated that. "You said you were close to cracking the case. Do you at least have any idea where we are? How did you find it?" she asked, her eyes round. She was surprised a guard hadn't come back for her yet, after all these questions. Perhaps they were preoccupied. Or perhaps Troy still had something to do with this.

"Oh you know. Went and found his file, sought out all the places in the city that I knew he owned."

"Wait. Why didn't you go to the police?" she half whispered the sentence in a desperate plea.

He looked up at her with drooping eyes. "Because I'm their number one suspect." Each word was carefully articulated.

She sighed. "So you know where we are?"

"Yes. I think so," he grunted.

She raised her hands. "Well?" Her eyes widened and she put her hands on her hips. *He's playing games. He likes having control over me.*

He mumbled something underneath his breath.

"What?" she asked.

"I said, come here and gimme some tongue, and I'll tell you."

"You disgust me."

He laughed, a raspy sound that turned into a small cough. He looked back up at her. "You want to know, or not?"

She looked around the room before she returned his stare. "I can't believe this," she whispered. She needed to know. Any information she could glean outside of what she already knew about this place could mean the difference between trapped and escape, death and life. "Why would you withhold information from me? What difference does it make to you?"

"Absolutely no difference." He laughed under his breath.

"You think this is funny?" She moved closer to him. As pathetic as he was, he still infuriated her.

"You better hurry. My time is limited."

She tilted her head in question.

"He made me swallow a pill. Told me, some sort of poison that would rupture my... " he coughed, "... internal organs."

She backed away from his chair. "Wha-you're bluffing."

He smirked. His sly smile was interrupted by another fit of coughs.

"Troy, please. Tell me! Tell me where we are so I know. You came here to find me, right? You came to help me escape?"

"I came for my kiss."

She slapped her thigh in rage and let out an exasperated sigh. She walked up to his chair. She stood and thought for a moment. *I could beat the information out of him.* But she was a lover, not a fighter. And he was pretty beaten already. She bent down to his face and looked him in the eyes. He parted his lips, revealing the small gap between his front teeth.

"You're all… " she whispered, looking at his swollen lip.

"Haven't you ever tasted a little blood before?" he slurred.

"I hate you." She swallowed hard, squeezed her eyes shut and moved in, reluctantly placing her lips on his.

He pushed his head forward and shoved his tongue between her lips. He tasted metallic.

She backed up quickly and wiped her mouth with the back of her hand, then spit onto the floor. "Ugh!"

"We're still in San Francisco. The city. This part of the building is concealed from the general public. There's people walking with shopping bags on their arms and coffees in their hands right underneath us."

"Do you know who the Warden is? Have you seen him?"

"Briefly. I was disoriented. Drugged." He coughed and looked at her. The red, broken blood vessels in his eyes were desperate. Blood sprayed from his mouth, into her face.

She gasped and fell against the door. She swiped her cheek with her hand and pulled it away to see the deep crimson smeared on her hand.

"When he forced the pill down… I told him to eat shit." His voice was soft.

She put her hand up to cover her mouth as Troy choked, blood spewing from his mouth and down his chin. She saw his eyes rolling into the back of his head before she covered her face and turned around. She banged her fists on the door. "Help! Let me out!"

The door flew open and she fell out into the hallway on her knees, face down at the feet of the guard.

"Get up. I said get up!" he yelled.

She used what energy she had left to get to her feet. She didn't dare look back in that room, and the guard slammed the door and grabbed her by her arm.

"What the hell happened? I leave for one second and-"

"I didn't do it."

The guard stopped in the hallway, pulled her to one side, and forced her to look at him. "You think that I think you're capable of something like that?"

She shook her head.

He let go and grabbed her arm again, pushing her back in the direction of the warehouse. "Now I have to clean that up," he muttered.

She thought she heard unsteadiness in his voice, but she couldn't tell over her own insecurity.

He unlocked the warehouse, pulled back the door, and pushed her in front of him.

Some of the people in the cages started murmuring. She soon found herself at hers.

"Raine? Oh my god, what happened? Are you okay?" Arie yelled from his cage, rage in his words.

"Not my blood," she whispered.

The guard opened the cage.

She bent down and crawled in.

The lock clicked shut behind her.

She hugged the cement with her hands, and rested her cheek on the cold concrete. She'd never be able to close her eyes without seeing that image of Troy in her mind, ever again.

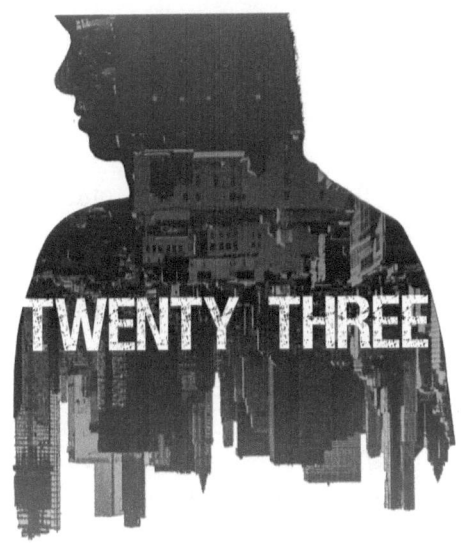

TWENTY THREE

"**R**aine." Arie's voice was soft on the other side of the wall. "You want to talk about it?"

She opened her mouth to speak, but no words came out. The blood that was caked on her skin had dried, and she felt it pulling at her face.

"Night guard dropped off our dinner a while back and you haven't touched it."

The thought of eating made her queasy. She moved to sit up and rubbed her stomach with both hands. "We're going to die." She found the words, though they sounded weak flowing off her tongue.

"Of course we're all going to die. We're humans. Unless you've found some fountain of youth nobody knows about?"

She wasn't up for jokes. She could tell he probably regretted it the moment the words came out of his mouth.

"No. Here. We're all going to die prisoners of the Warden." She spoke in a monotone.

"C'mon now. You sound like the other hopelesses in the cages around us would if they ever said anything. I know some bad things happened to you here Raine, but you can't give up. There's gotta be a way."

She looked up to see his hand outside the bars, stretching out to her. She reached up to it and wrapped her hand around his fingers, giving them a gentle squeeze before she let go. "I'm not feeling very well," she whispered, whether he heard her or not.

It wasn't long before she heard the echo of boots on the concrete outside her cell. The sound stopped in front of her cage. *They're probably picking up the food I didn't eat,* she thought, exhausted. When the boots didn't walk away, she raised her head up and looked over her shoulder.

It was the nice guard. The one that freed her from the leather table. He'd knelt down and looked in her cage. When he saw her stir, he nearly lost his balance. He hopped back up and bent down to unlock her cage.

She didn't move.

"C'mon," he coaxed her.

She groaned. "I don't wanna go to any more rooms," she mumbled.

"Did I say you had a choice?" His voice was stern.

It surprised her. She hadn't heard anything but kindness from this man since she arrived, when he did decide to speak.

She sighed deeply and pulled herself up to a seated position, turning around.

When he saw her, his hand went to his stomach, and his face turned as white as a ghost.

"I know," she said, as her eyes prickled with tears.

"Come on. Get out."

She crawled out of the cage and used what energy she had to push off the floor and stand. She turned her head and looked into Arie's cage. She only saw the bottom of his bare dirty feet, the rest of his body in shadow. She walked, one foot in front of the other, out of the warehouse with the guard behind her.

"Right," he directed her.

"Not going that way?" she asked, motioning the opposite direction.

"No."

"I've never been this way before."

"I'm taking you to the guards quarters."

"Is that allowed?" If it had been any other guard, she'd be punished for asking this. But it was different with this one. They shared the connection of knowing the truth about this operation.

"He's out."

She stopped. "Out? Well then why don't we just le-"

"Quiet!" he snapped. "You can't just be shouting those things out around here! There's eyes everywhere, don't you get it?"

She mashed herself against the wall, wide eyed. "I'm sor-"

"Save it." He grabbed her by the wrist and guided her down the hallway, to a door on the left that he needed to unlock. The key was stuck at first and he had to jiggle it to get it loose. The door opened and she went in; he followed and locked the door behind him. They were in a sort of closet, with a staircase behind.

She hesitated before going down the stairs. "Are the other guards down there?" she asked.

He shook his head. "No. Night and Day guards have different quarters. I think it's so we can't talk together. And Granger is out on duty, doing our checklist."

The no nonsense guard's name was Granger. "You guys were given a checklist?"

"No. We made it for ourselves. We weren't given anything but a uniform, a role, and a threat." He put his hand out to guide her down the stairs.

She turned and followed the wall down the spiral staircase, yet another nook in this labyrinth. "This is creepy," she whispered back at him.

"The problem with this place is that there's always a way in, and no way out. It's easier to keep tabs on people that way. And you don't know where there's a camera. Sometimes they're obvious, sometimes you can't even tell if they're there or not."

She moved out of the way while he leaned forward, unlocked the door, and pushed it open.

She entered and saw two camping cots on opposite walls, with a desk in between. There were no windows—like the rest of the rooms in this place, except for the white loft of course—and the small room reminded her of the dorms she was forced to pay $900 per month to live in when she was a freshman.

"Why did you bring me here?" she asked.

"You need to clean that off you. I saw the scene. Nobody deserves that."

She looked down. "He wasn't a good guy. But he came here for me. And now he's-that was horrible. You're right. Nobody deserves that."

He gave an airy laugh. "You're right. But what I meant was, nobody deserves to see what you had to see."

She looked up at him. She couldn't imagine the way Troy must have looked, like straight out of a horror film, maybe, judging by the way her skin felt with his blood caked on it.

"Straight back there there's a bathroom." He pointed to the open door in the back. "You can shower in there. I'll wait out here for you. But make it quick, okay?"

She nodded and went to the door in the back of the room. She creaked it open. It wasn't luxurious, that was for sure. But then again, it almost was. It was a private room with four walls. It was a shower with an actual shower head on it, not just a pipe or a skin-peeling jet. There was a sink and a private toilet. He was right, she'd most definitely prefer to be a guard, as opposed a prisoner.

She pulled off the stiff gown and dropped it on the floor. The knobs were standard, and she adjusted it to a comfortable temperature. Another luxury she'd taken for granted before. Water temperature. She had a choice. She stepped into the shower and pulled the sliding door closed. The moment the water flowed over her tangled hair and face, she closed her eyes and heaved a large sigh. She reached down and grabbed a bottle of soap. As she squeezed a small amount into her hand, the smell of spearmint and pine wafted her nose. It smelled masculine, but it smelled like something other than blood, sweat, and neglect, so she rubbed it into her hair.

If we act like there are cameras on us at all times, the Warden will never have an accurate depiction of human behavior. Even though this is as real as real gets, we'll make decisions based on what we think he wants us to do, not what we would normally do. The whole experiment is skewed. Fixed. For the outcome that the psychopath wants.

She wrung her hair out with her hands. Soapy suds swirled around the drain at her feet. And though she wished she could stay in there longer and just let the water flow over her, the guard told her to make it quick. She was grateful for any amount of time she got. She turned off the knobs and pulled the fogged up door sideways. A gray towel hung on a hook. She grabbed it and patted her body. It felt nice to have something clean to dry with, and even though the fabric was thin and rough, she didn't care. She dried off her body and put the towel on her head. She rubbed her hair and hung the towel back up on the hook.

Stepping out onto the concrete, she looked down at her folded up gown on the floor. It was stained with blood. Troy's blood. Her stomach felt queasy as her exhausted eyes welled up once more. She couldn't contain the weight she felt in her chest. *No human deserved the fate that he got. And I thought he was lying about it, bluffing.*

She reached up and swiped at her eyes, patting her tender cheekbones. Then she tiptoed over to the door and cracked it open.

"Hey-" It was then that she realized she didn't even know the nice guard's name. She just thought of him as "nice guard." "Do you have any more uniforms out there? Mine's um… " She heard him stir.

"Yeah. Hang on." More shuffling. "It's not washed. Somebody else wore it before you, but it's cleaner than yours." He handed it to her.

She slipped her arm through the crack in the door and grabbed the gown from him, then closed the bathroom door again. She slipped it on over her head and looked into the mirror above the sink. This one hit her right at the knee, as opposed to the gown she had before, which was well up on her thigh. She preferred this one. She wouldn't think about who wore it before her.

She leaned toward the mirror and looked at her face. She looked different. Her eyes were stony and grave. Her hairline was still bruised purple and blue, and her eyes bore sunken blue half moons underneath them. She reached up and touched her cheeks. Her lips were pale, and she wasn't sure if it was her imagination or not, but her cheeks looked thinner—no doubt the result of eating cold mush for days.

She turned and swung the door open.

The nice guard was sitting on his cot.

"What's your name?" she asked softly.

He looked up at her. "Perez. I'm sorry I didn't share that with you sooner."

"We've been mostly preoccupied." She smiled at him. "So, you know this room isn't bugged?" she asked, looking around. Surely he wouldn't be comfortable being here with her if he thought he was being watched.

"I don't think so. My partner and I have talked about stuff in here and there's been no repercussions. I think he's more interested in other things. I think he's just satisfied to see us doing our duties up in the warehouse, he doesn't care what we do in our free time, really. It's almost ominous. Hey, grab that comb in the bathroom—I'll brush your hair if you want."

She was caught off guard. "You want to brush my hair?"

"I mean, I don't have to. I just thought you'd like your hair untangled."

She turned and went back into the humid bathroom, grabbed the comb off the sink, and returned. She walked over to the cot and sat in front of him. She did enjoy having her hair touched. The circumstances were unusual, but she didn't complain. She handed him the comb and looked straight ahead.

He ran the comb through her hair, careful not to pull on it when he came to tangles. They sat in silence while he combed through each strand, smoothing it down her back.

She closed her eyes as he combed. It was another luxury. She felt chills when he grazed her ear.

He set the comb down on the cot and separated her hair into three sections at the scalp. "I used to French braid my little girl's hair all the time," he said, weaving her hair back and forth, and pulling other pieces of hair into the braid as he went.

"You miss her."

"With every single breath I take," he said. "Josie. That's her name." He finished up the braid. "Look. I brought you down here because I want to let you in on my plan. I think you're my only hope of getting out of here. Of all the people I've seen come through here, I see it in you. You're strong. Strong up here."

She turned around to see him pointing to his head. "So what are we going to do?" she asked.

"I'm going to take you back to your cage. Tomorrow night, Megan is going to distract the Warden, and I'll be able to drop the keys by your cell. You should be able to reach your hands through and grab them, let yourself out. I highly, highly suggest you go alone. I understand you'll probably want to rescue others. But the only way this can work—the only way we can slip through the cracks, is if you act alone."

Her stomach flopped. *Arie.* "I don't know if I-"

"Raine. It's the only way. Please understand this."

She closed her lips and looked down at the cot.

"At the end of the hallway upstairs, the last door at the end is a set of stairs that lead to the yard. Not the way you went last time, okay?"

She nodded her understanding.

"I'm going to unlock that door earlier, before I drop the keys. So when you pass by the door to these quarters, I need you to drop the keys inside the door. I'll need them back, or else I'll get burned for not having my set and he'll know I was involved. Do you understand?"

She nodded. "Yes."

"Can I trust you? If you want to save us, you have to get out yourself."

"What's in the yard? How do I escape from there?" she asked.

"Well I'm hoping there's a fire escape up there you can climb down."

She nodded. "Okay. I can climb."

"Can you remember all the moving parts?" he asked, standing up and moving to the door. He motioned for her to follow. "I have to take you back."

She stood, reluctant to go. "Yes. Tomorrow night?"

"Tomorrow night."

It seemed so final. She hesitated. "I have one more question."

He nodded.

"Why not you? You have the keys, you're not locked up. Why don't you run? It just seems so much easier."

He was quiet a moment, and he leaned against the doorjamb. A crease appeared between his eyes and he reached up and scratched his chin. "I've thought about that, no doubt. You say I'm not locked up. Not physically, like you. But I am without a doubt imprisoned. I can't risk my family. I just can't take the chance of getting caught trying to escape, and the consequences of that. I'm sorry… that makes it seem like your life isn't as important and that's not true. But you stand a better chance."

She watched him squirm. Somehow his body language told her that he'd been thinking about this question for quite a long time.

"Where my family keeps me alive, and the thought of getting back to them is everything to me, they're also the reason I'm still here." He looked away.

"I understand," she whispered.

He put his hand on the doorknob. "My name is Brandon Perez. When you escape—not if, but when—can you make sure my wife and baby know that you saw me alive and that I love them? I think of them with every waking breath."

Raine felt a tug of emotion behind her eyes. She nodded. "Yes. I'll tell them Brandon. I promise. And I promise I'll come back and get every last one of you out of here."

He nodded and patted her on the arm before he turned and made his way back up the stairs.

Raine followed close behind.

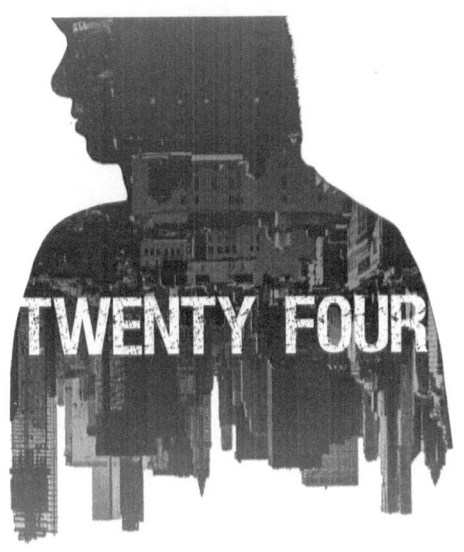

TWENTY FOUR

She watched as Perez walked away from her cage, and up the long aisle. She heard a low murmur between guards by the door before the voices, and the light from the hallway, vanished into the shadow. It was already nighttime in the warehouse. The darkness was to get their minds set that it was time for their biological clock to recognize rest or sleep. Though the constant fear loomed over them, that they could be woken up at obscene hours for drill exercises or surprise field trips to the other rooms in the maze prison.

Whenever the black overtook the warehouse and skewed her long distance vision, her other senses were heightened, and she could identify pipes knocking and air vents kicking on. She was grateful it was dark, so the other inmates couldn't see her cleaned up. She was afraid they'd think she was getting special treatment again, or that perhaps she'd had to trade to get a clean gown. She didn't like those thoughts either.

Though somebody else didn't need to see her to know she'd gotten a chance to clean up. He spoke through the darkness, "You smell like Meg." His voice was calm, quiet, and judgmental.

She didn't respond at first. She wasn't sure what he meant by that.

"Pine. Spearmint. Guilt."

She inhaled as quietly as she could. *What is he talking about?* She felt defensive, and she recoiled back to the corner of her cage and drew her knees into her chest. *He's intuitive,* she thought. She did feel guilty. Guilty that Perez had a plan for escape. *Guilty that the plan did not include Arie.* In fact, it purposely excluded Arie, if it was going to be successful.

"That's not fair." She finally spoke, her voice low. "You haven't even given me time to think about what just happened."

"I'm sorry. It's just... me sitting in here and not knowing where they've taken you or what's happening. Well it's the worst feeling imaginable."

She slumped again. "No, I'm sorry." She turned around and lay down in the cage. She rested her head on the bars, and turned on her side to face Arie's wall. She didn't have to ask him to come close. She heard his breathing.

"Arie," she whispered. She wanted to see if he could hear her.

"I'm here," he whispered back. His face was just as close to the cage as hers.

She closed her eyes and smiled. "There's a plan."

There was a silence between them. "You know I'm always up for a good plan."

When she heard the boyish grin on his lips, she knew there was no way around this. She knew that Arie was coming with her, and he'd be by her side the entire time.

After she was finished telling him the plan, and the fact that Perez told her it'd be unsuccessful if she didn't act alone, the two of them lay in their cages, their hands through the bars, fingers laced together.

"Thank you for confiding in me, Raine. You didn't have to do that."

She smiled. "If I escape, you escape."

"I like that better than 'If I can't escape, you can't.'"

For the rest of the night, she ran the plan over and over in her head. It would have been smart to get as much sleep as she could so she would have a full and alert brain tomorrow, but she was too nervous to close her eyes.

As a therapist, she'd been trained to always be the one in control. This last week, or a week of which she could remember, was the biggest nightmare of her life. She was sick of being the one out of control and out of the decisions she was supposed to make for herself.

Tonight, would be the last night she'd spend at the mercy of the psychopath.

TWENTY FIVE

So much for trying to get any sleep tonight, she thought as she lay awake in the cage and stared at the ceiling. She drifted for just a moment; a dreamless, restless sleep, before she jolted awake again, thinking she'd slept through the morning.

She hadn't. It was still dark inside the warehouse. She lay awake and listened to Arie's long, heavy breathing.

His breathing patterns were relaxing and it brought her into a sort of awakened meditative state. A chill crawled up her spine as she thought about lying on the table at the hands of the narcissistic psychopath. She inhaled and exhaled, focusing on her breathing and allowing her thoughts to explore different parts of her mind.

When she was on that table, he mentioned the will to survive, that it was ingrained in humans.

She imagined how heartbroken her mom and dad must be since they thought she died in the car wreck. To think of them coping with their reality of having to bury their child. The child is not supposed to die before the parent.

She put the palm of her hand on her chest to match her heartbeat up with the pace of Arie's breathing. Though even that soothing pattern couldn't comfort her, and a lump formed in her throat. *Because of me, their entire lives were probably uprooted. What if Dad left his good job at the law firm, or stopped his favorite pastime of gardening? What if Mom's heart was so heavy she stopped eating and grew thin?*

And her sister. *Chloe. Chloe has always looked up to me. Looked up to my independence, and dedication.* She talked about moving out to San Francisco once she got enough money saved up.

Maybe I should have gone back to Ohio when I graduated. Why did I have to be so far away from my family? She sighed.

I have people here that need me too. She was a life coach to many clients that needed guidance through the stress and anxiety that life could bring. Not only did she help them cope, but also they helped her. Here she was, a person who encompassed more paranoia and anxiety than even some of the souls that came to her for help. Her clients' progress showed her that there was hope for her as well. She found fulfillment in seeing others succeed and not just survive.

She needed to succeed here too, succeed in escaping this prison and getting her life back.

Perhaps after she got out of here, she'd go back home to Ohio for a while and recuperate. Or maybe after this nightmare was over, she could go on a vacation, a getaway. Or maybe she should just go back to her apartment with her pup Viona, and live her life normally again.

Though she wasn't able to comprehend how she'd ever be able to live her life normally again after what happened here. Raine was lucky that she met Brandon Perez, who claimed her from the guards from the start, which ultimately protected her from being harmed. Perhaps they thought he was taking advantage of her, or treating her the way the Warden wanted, but he was a gentleman. And he was ultimately going to be her ticket out. She was thankful for Arie, who had been there for her from the moment they put her in here. Arie represented her sanity. He was the reason she wasn't falling to the wayside, or existing in her cage as a vegetable, the way she'd seen many other prisoners.

She thought about the other prisoners as well. She had never interacted with them. But each and every person, male and female, in those cages around her, had a story. They all led their own lives before they were stolen from them. The charade of keeping them in dog cages, for one, was pure torture. Depriving them of basic needs. Sleep, little to no food, basic comfort, privacy, choice. It's no wonder the others were in a sort of coma. It was their defense mechanism. In some ways, it was smart. Comply. Blend in. Don't bring attention to yourself.

Raine had chosen quite the opposite. She had done nothing but make a racket since she got there. She was a new hope to the troublemakers and double agents that were already there inside the prison—Arie and Megan and Perez. She'd already attempted an escape and seen the Warden's living space, something that she hadn't even told Arie about yet. Lastly, the fact that she'd seen the face of her kidnapper.

Nothing good could come from that. He was used to living behind cameras. Used to living a double life.

She'd seen his face now, which meant if she escaped, she could turn him in to authorities and give a pretty accurate description. This scared her even more. That meant that the Warden was even more vulnerable. That meant that he had no intention of Raine ever seeing the light of day again.

And that, to her, was the most frightening reality of all.

TWENTY SIX

Mornings in Altruism Prison came abruptly, in the form of the warehouse fluorescents blinking on. Raine squirmed on the concrete; stiffness gripped her neck and shoulders. She felt as though she'd just shut her eyes a moment ago. The light in her eyes told her one thing, it was the next day, the day she would implement Perez's plan for her escape. All she needed to do was make it through today. Survive one last shift of the daytime guards.

The door to the warehouse opened, almost like clockwork. She moved to the front of her cage and peered down the aisle. She held her breath, she wasn't sure which one of the guards would come in.

She felt like one of Pavlov's dogs every time the door squealed open. It was the result of classical conditioning. No matter who came through those doors, the moment she heard them, her stomach twisted with anxiety.

This time it was the quiet guard. Buck's partner. He carried a large stack of plastic bowls that looked similar to the ones her parents used while camping in one of those pop up campers when she was a kid.

He dropped the bowls one by one on the ground in front of the cage doors. A clatter echoed from each bowl as it landed. He finished up the row and walked back out of the warehouse door.

"How'd you sleep?" Arie asked.

"Didn't." Her voice was groggy.

"Oh, you too?"

"Big day."

They were quiet a moment.

The quiet guard made his way back down the row, carrying a pot this time.

"You know what I'm really craving this morning?" Arie asked.

"Hm?"

"Some nice, cold, soggy oatmeal."

Raine stifled a laugh.

The guard slopped the usual mashed oatmeal cereal into the bowls.

"Hey, look. It's your lucky day," she whispered as the guard approached.

He stopped in front of their cages, and dropped some oatmeal into Arie's bowl.

Raine looked up at him. He stared down at her, his eyes beet red and he slowly poured her ladle of slop into the bowl. He didn't blink.

Does he know something? She looked away from him, down to the floor. Submission.

He moved on.

She exhaled. When the guard was down the row, she reached through the bars and grabbed the bowl. Unless she wanted to scoop it up and bring it to her face through the bars, she learned to put her hand on top of the oatmeal and tip the bowl to its side, then slide it vertically through the bars before setting it down flat again. With her hand already covered with the stuff, she scooped up the sloppy mush and brought it to her lips. It was cold as usual, apart from the time she was in solitary confinement and Megan brought her the warm bowl. Best to swallow it without chewing, or else the texture and the temperature would make her gag. She needed to get it down and have something substantial settle in her nervous stomach. At least they were fed at all.

She closed her eyes as she swallowed the cold, lumpy oatmeal and imagined it was a mason jar of gluten free, cinnamon apple, honey, overnight oats that she'd just pulled from the fridge. She licked her lips and scooped another bite into her mouth with her fingers.

The guard was back, picking up empty bowls as he walked the aisle.

She hurried up and shoved the rest in her mouth, licked the inside of the bowl the best she could, and slipped it sideways through the bars, onto the floor.

The guard scooped it up as it landed, and continued on.

She watched as he crossed over to the other side, opposite her. He picked up each bowl and added it to the stack.

He stopped short at one of the cages diagonal to hers. A guy with a bald head and tattoos covering both of his arms sat slumped in the cage. The guard looked in at the bowl, and moved onto the next. That guy must not have touched his food. The guard left it and continued to the rest, leaving with the stack.

That wasn't good. They needed to eat, especially if they'd been holding out for a while. She wasn't sure how long he'd been doing this. She'd never even done something as small as saying hi to this guy, and she'd passed his cage several times as she was brought in and out.

She went over the plan again in her head: which door would be unlocked already, and where to drop Perez's keys. Just when she was about to settle and get as comfortable as physically possible in the back of her cage, the door opened again. Anxiety.

Buck walked in.

She hoped he wasn't headed in her direction.

He wasn't. He was headed for the single bowl lying on the concrete. He walked over to the tattooed man's cage. "You not hungry?" he asked, leaning down. "Ah I see how it is." He put his key into the cage, and instructed to the quiet guard to bring the guy out. The man was limp, and dragged easily out of the cage, his limbs flopping like a dead fish. The partner dropped him on the floor by Buck's feet.

Buck knelt down and grabbed the bowl, scooping a big handful of the goop. "Yer gone eat this, whether you like it or not, you ungrateful lil prick." He shoved the food into the man's mouth, and covered it with his hand.

Raine covered her own mouth and pushed back in her cage, her whole body tense.

The man tried to move his head back and forth, choking underneath the pressing hand. His eyes were wide.

Raine tore her eyes from the scene and curled into a ball. She thought she felt the oatmeal working its way back up her throat, along with some acid, but she swallowed it back down and tried to take herself away from the scene.

She opened her eyes again when she heard the flailing. As soon as the guard took his hand away and the man had choked down the mush that was pasted across his mouth and face, Buck placed his hand on the back of the guy's head and smashed it into the bowl on the concrete. His head bounced, and blood gushed from his face.

"Put em back," he called to his partner. The quiet guard shuffled, dragging the unconscious man, who was bleeding from the nose. He tossed him back into the cage, closed the door behind him, and locked it.

"Anyone else not hungry?" he shouted out to the rest of them, his voice resonating through the warehouse. He pulled out his baton from his belt. As he walked down the row of cages, he dragged his bat across the bars.

The sound was deafening; the pattern of the banging baton on metal, *clang clang clang clang*.

It wasn't until the guards were gone and the sound subsided that Raine took her hands off her ears. But she didn't have the guts to open her eyes to see what was left of breakfast.

TWENTY SEVEN

Raine ran her fingers through her hair, unraveling the French braid. The crimped hair hung down her back, and she rested her head up against Arie's wall. If she hadn't been kidnapped, she never would have met him. *Do I feel close to him because of the circumstances? Would I have looked at him twice on the street?*

After they escaped, would she want to see him? Or would it remind her of the horrors of this prison? Would the relationship be healthy if the foundation had been built upon the terror of their experience?

"Arie, what are you doing over there?"

He shuffled over. "I'm trying to sleep the day away. Sleep makes the night come faster. We need our strength."

"I can't sleep."

"Talk to me, then."

She smiled. "I don't want to bother you."

"It's ok. I want to be bothered. Tell me about Viona."

Viona... she smiled to herself at the sound of her name. "She has an intuition stronger than any animal I've ever seen. She knows when I'm lonely or sad. She'd come and put her black, wet, nose on my knee until I called her up on the couch to cuddle me. But she'd wait to see if that's what I needed first, like she knew. I don't know. It's crazy."

"What kind of dog is she?"

"Some kind of Pit Bull mix. She's light colored. A creamy tan color. I miss her."

"Was she a rescue?"

"Yeah. I adopted her from a shelter, but she was born there."

"Ah, I see. I don't think I could choose between my dogs. Like I said, there's about thirty or so in the shelter, but we get more dropped off all the time. The best times are when they have a microchip or something, finding their worried owners that have been searching everywhere for them. The worst is when they've been just dumped somewhere. Abandoned. Dogs don't judge. They see and feel and experience everything in this world at an exponential rate, but their lives are just so short that they don't have time to remain angry or judgmental. Unless they've been abused. Then they get smart. Defensive. You have to gain their trust."

His voice was boyish and she held onto every word. *He really loves his work.* Even if it didn't seem like owning a shelter was such a glamorous profession. Even if he didn't go to college and spend thousands of dollars getting into debt to get there, like she did.

"When I get back, I want to take away the cages in the shelter. Not take away their boundaries or structure, but the rows of kennels. We let them out for runs and play time, and we also have lots of blankets and comfort in the kennels, but sometimes I feel like being here has opened up a whole new perspective for me. I'm in this terrible dream. Like this is a metaphor for what I'm doing."

"You can't blame yourself for this. This—this is the work of a psychopath. The man is ill, demented. But he has this idea that he feels like he's doing something right for the world. Of course it's at our expense, but people like him need to be identified, they need to be helped."

"Are you defending him?"

"I didn't say that!"

"I know, I'm teasing. Did you learn all that in your profession?"

"Yes. I've worked with monsters before. And I know there are many more out there who have never been treated. Even after dedicating my life to studying the human mind and human behavior, despite spending all my waking hours trying to help people, I still ended up in this cage. It's sort of, I don't know. Ironic?"

"So what are you in for?" Arie asked.

Raine was quiet a moment. "What did they say I did?"

"Yeah."

"They say I murdered someone. Second degree? You heard them when they threw me in here."

"Well I don't know. I think I was disoriented. Mesmerized by your beauty and resilience when I saw them drag you in."

She laughed.

"Did you… did you start to believe what they accused you of?" he asked.

"In the beginning, yes. It's only natural. I was distressed, and in these shocking circumstances. You don't expect to be a prisoner in a prison that was built from scratch at the hands of a psychopath, or you shouldn't. I bet you there are other victims in here that still think they're in an actual jail. But we know this is highly unorthodox. And I didn't tell you what happened to me the first time I escaped."

"I was afraid to ask. I've heard Meg's stories, at least in the beginning. She's stopped sharing."

She stretched her neck from side to side. "Well to be brief, I wandered into the residence of our Warden. I'm not entirely sure the guards have even seen it. But for some reason the door to get down to his loft was unlocked. I bet you he didn't expect anybody to come down there, because we're all locked up. Or supposed to be."

"Or maybe he did want someone to come down there. Maybe he expected it and he was luring you into some kind of trap." Arie said.

"Well I did think that at one point, too. But the way he acted when he captured me... as if I'd caught him off guard and he had to do something to gain back the feeling of control and power over me. He kept using that anesthetic syringe as a threat on me. It was terrifying. But he didn't hurt me fully, Arie."

"What did his place look like?"

"Sterile. It was completely clean and white. No personal effects. Modern decor. Huge windows."

"What did you see?"

"Sunlight. It was so bright and I was disoriented from my eyes being so used to the dark. You know, like when you've been playing outside for a while and you come inside and your eyes need time to adjust—everything is all dark? Well this is sort of the opposite effect. Only I didn't have time to adjust, because I heard a noise."

"Did you find where he has all his camera feeds?"

"I did not. Can I ask *you* something now?" she asked. He was quiet, and she took that as a yes. "What were *you* accused of when they brought you here?"

"Animal endangerment." His voice was low and monotone, as if that were the worst crime you could possibly commit.

"Did you ask me if I started to believe what they accused me of, because you did?" she asked. The barrier between them was beginning to get to her. She wished she could see him face to face. The wall blocked her from seeing his body language, one of her favorite things to observe when she had a conversation with someone. She tried to tell herself to shut off the psychologist. It was only natural, after all her training, to diagnose all of her friends and family. In this situation, there was nothing to figure out. She punished herself in her mind.

But the fact that the wall stood between them forced her to listen to his words with her ears, as opposed to her eyes. And she heard the tinges of emotion in his words, the sincerity. For now, that had to be enough. She felt like she herself needed a therapist to bring her out of this mess in her mind.

"Yes. I did," he replied, "I racked my brain and came up with scenarios that connected me to this place. There was one time. The shelter is full of volunteers, right? Well we have some volunteers come in and walk the dogs, give them exercise. We rescued a mutt that was chained in a backyard and neglected for years. We hadn't had the opportunity to work with him yet. Well one of the volunteers went into his cage to get him out—also a big no no. You're supposed to make the dog come to you, not approach them. Anyway, he mauled her. I did the only thing I could to save the poor girl. She needed thirty stitches. And I had to bury the dog myself."

She swallowed hard. She didn't dare ask what he did to the animal. "But you had to. You had to save the girl."

"But did I take it too far? Could I have saved her without killing the dog? It wasn't his fault. He'd been abused by humans his whole life. He didn't understand what was going on. I've had a lot of time to think in here about this stuff."

"Me too." she agreed. "We're in this together, man. I'm like you. I searched my memories for something I could have possibly done to get myself here. As a therapist, there were many emotionally unstable people I was supposed to help. But I couldn't help everyone. There was this one boy... he... he committed suicide. And I believed it was my fault because I couldn't save him. He came to me for help and I failed."

"No."

"Just listen. I understand that it wasn't my fault he took his own life. But I can't help but feel responsible for it. Everyone makes choices. In the moment, you have to decide which one is the right one, and which one is the wrong one. Sometimes, you just have to go with instinct. And those are the moments, when we don't really have time to think, that define us."

"So what kind of person are you?" he asked quietly.

"I'm resilient."

"Lets get the hell out of here, Raine."

She nodded, even though he couldn't see her. "Lets get the hell out of here," she whispered back.

TWENTY EIGHT

When the lights went out in the warehouse, Raine's heart skipped a beat. It was night. It was time. She'd run the plan over and over in her head so many times that the blueprint was engraved in her mind.

Her nerves had already begun to run marathons through her limbs, and she rubbed at her cramped stomach. She looked up and down the row at the inmates, no more than shadows in their cages. Her hyperawareness pulled at her, and her eyes grew itchy with tiredness. She didn't dare give in to it.

The worst part was that she had no idea when Perez was going to come. She'd waited all day, what felt like the longest day of her life, and now she wasn't sure how long she'd have to wait in the dark for the plan to start.

She stretched down to her legs. It'd been at least a day since she'd stood up. It'd probably been longer for some of the other victims, and that she regretted, but both legs tingled and grew numb, so she shook them and stretched, twisting her spine from side to side.

As the time passed, the uneasiness that swirled in her stomach increased. *Something went wrong. Some-*

thing had to have gone wrong. He'd have been there by now. Just when she thought she'd explode, the door creaked open. No nonsense guard, Perez's night shift partner, stepped in, tucking his disheveled shirt into his pants. He yanked his waistband up and pulled out the ring of keys. He walked down the aisle, stopping at each cage and tugging on the padlocks attached to each.

He's checking the locks, she observed, her nerves wound up so tight she might vomit. "What the hell is going on?" she whispered over to Arie

The guard looked up. "Who's talking?"

Raine shrunk back up into her cage as quietly as she could.

He finished checking the lock on the tattooed man's cage, the cage whose shadow hadn't moved since this morning. "There's going to be some changes around here." His boots made a clicking noise every time he stepped down on the concrete. "Added security. Less... leeway."

She'd never heard Brandon's roommate speak this much before. But he was one to follow the rules, that was certain. She'd seen that much, hence the nickname "no nonsense guard."

"One of my duties is checking to see that none of your cages have been breached."

"How do you expect our cages to be breached?" a rough voice asked, a voice Raine hadn't heard before.

The guard took his baton out of his utility belt and smacked the cage, rattling it and all those around it. "Shut it." He wasn't as loud and obnoxious as the day guard, but it was still enough to scare everyone. He continued to go from cage to cage and rattled each lock. Nobody else spoke. When he reached Raine's cage, he bent down and tugged at her padlock.

She couldn't help but look into his face, the whites of her eyes glowing in her cage.

"He's not coming." His lips formed the words, and he didn't need to vocalize them for her to lip read.

Her stomach flipped. Her throat tightened. She wanted to ask questions, but he'd already moved onto the next cage.

TWENTY NINE

She hadn't heard from Arie. She hadn't heard from Perez. The warehouse was pitch black. She lay in her cage, anxiety controlling every inch of her. Her eyes were wide, and her breathing was short and quick, causing dizziness. Raine moved to the front of her cage and wrapped her fingers around the bars, peering up and down the row. What was she supposed to do if their plan was foiled?

And then she heard the soft patter of feet on the concrete. Her heart beat with every step. Megan knelt down in front of Arie's cage and unlocked the padlock.

Raine saw Arie appear. He held his hand up to his mouth, leaned in, and whispered into Megan's ear. She shook her head, and they turned to Raine.

Raine was so startled she couldn't formulate words in her mind, let alone speak. She noticed Megan was wearing regular clothing, jeans and a dark t-shirt.

For a moment, Raine was suspicious. Why was Megan wearing normal clothes and not the inmate outfit? Was she an inside job? Whose side was she on? Why did she get these privileges that nobody else did? Did Raine *want* to know the answer to that question?

Megan fiddled with her lock, careful not to make a noise, to wake any of the other prisoners.

"What's goin-"

Megan put her delicate finger up to her mouth. She shook her head no, her eyes wide, and motioned Raine to come out of the cage. Arie stood behind Megan. When she cleared the bars, Arie took her hand and they headed down the aisle.

A shrill scream erupted from their right.

Raine jumped.

One of the prisoners screamed bloody murder, banged on the cage, and rattled the door.

Megan ran up to the cage and hit it with her hand. "Shhh... please... shut up!"

"If I can't get out, you can't get out. If I can't get out, you can't get-"

"He's crazy. Go! Just go." Megan led them towards the door.

Before they reached it, the alarm went off. The sound was similar to the one that sounded when victims were taken from their cages and disappeared through the door. The noise repeated over and over, pounding in her head, and she felt the prickling of anxiety. She clutched Arie's hand tighter, and they leaped over the threshold. She looked back to see Megan in their wake.

Megan slammed the door closed. The alarm was still audible in the hallway, but fainter. They took off down the hall past the guards quarters door. It was shut. Raine let go of Arie's hand and reached out. She rattled the locked handle. She looked up at Arie in front of her, his brow furrowed.

"Guards quarters. Something must have happened to Perez."

"Go!" Megan whispered, pushing them both down towards the end of the hallway.

They picked up the pace.

Raine looked ahead of them, and it felt as though the door at the end of the hallway grew further and further away.

When they reached the door, Arie tugged onto the knob. Locked.

Her heart pounded, and she gasped for air, almost out of energy. She bent down with her hands on her knees to catch her breath. She felt Arie's strong hand on her back.

Generally she was fit. She did yoga and ran with Viona often. Her time in the prison sucked all of her energy. Her adrenaline surge was ebbing away.

Megan pushed in front of them, looking over her shoulder constantly. She tried a key from the ring, shaking as she tried to insert it. It didn't work. She tried the next.

Raine kept looking back down the hall.

Arie put his hand on Megan's arm, "It's okay. You can do this, Meg. You're a hero right now."

She tried the next key. It slid into the lock. She turned and pulled the door open.

A burst of cool air greeted them, and she pulled open the door to reveal a stone staircase that led to the sky.

It was the first time in a while that Raine had felt the outside air on her face. The gust of wind smelled fresh, and open. Arie walked through the door, with Raine following close behind, but Megan stood back.

Raine looked at her.

She stood there, the prison behind her. Her red hair was stark in the light, and it shadowed her soft, pale face.

"C'mon, Meg!" Arie reached out to her.

Raine felt a tinge of mistrust again, and she wasn't sure why.

Megan had just set them free. But how did she get the keys? And why was she wearing jeans and a shirt instead of the gowns they were forced to wear, or her scrubs?

"I have to go back to the Warden," she squeaked.

"What the hell are you talking about?" Arie hissed at her.

"For you two to go free—I have to go back to him. I have to make it look like you broke out on your own. I don't know what happened to Perez. I think the other guards caught wind of what was going on and they chickened out. But there's not much time!" The alarm was still audible behind her.

Raine looked at her, though Megan only looked at Arie.

"This is the only way," she said. Her soft features looked defeated. She was gentle. Delicate. "There is no life for me out there. If I stay, and I do what he wants, he's not... " It was as if she couldn't form the words. "... he's not that bad."

Raine opened her mouth to protest, but shut it again. Her mind ran wild with explanations as to why Megan acted this way. It was obvious she was under the Warden's manipulation, but there was no other coping mechanism. She needed to be that way in order to survive. But the fact that the chance to escape was presented to her, and she refused to take it in efforts to save the others, was heroic.

This entire time she hadn't been sure what side Megan was on, what game she was playing, whether or not she was even one of the prisoners or if she had a bigger ulterior motive. Though now it seemed clear. It appeared that Megan was kidnapped so long ago, she felt like Arie and Raine still had a chance but she didn't. It wasn't so bad for her inside the jail, and perhaps her only chance of escape was if Arie and Raine could get out and possibly bust the whole charade.

Arie stepped down a few stairs, past Raine and towards Megan.

Raine watched them as Arie drew close to Megan.

"I *will* come back for you. Okay? You got that?" he asked her.

"I know you will," she whispered.

Raine's eyes prickled with tears. She was grateful to Megan, for the risk she took to help them. She turned away from the prison hallway and looked up to the top of the stairs, which was marked by white puffy clouds crossing the sky.

As she turned to climb, the door to the guards' quarters burst open.

It all happened so fast. Buck appeared from behind the door and grabbed Megan's hair, yanking her back into a chokehold. Arie leaped at him.

The guard had his gun pointed at Megan's head.

Arie stepped back with his arms up. "Go Raine!" he screamed over his shoulder.

She hesitated and looked up at the roof. Now was her chance-quite possibly her only chance.

She whipped her head back to see Buck with his gun pressed to Megan's temple. She saw Megan's jaw clench. Her eyes were narrowed, watching everything that happened in front of her.

Raine stood, frozen. She wasn't sure what she should do, what could she control, which had always been very little within these walls.

"What do you want?" Arie remained with his hands in the air.

Raine faced Arie's back. She thought she saw his knees shaking, as if he'd collapse at any moment.

"I wantchu back in yer damn cages."

She remained on the stairs. They were wasting too much time. Megan had been gone for too long, and surely the Warden would be looking at his cameras by now.

Both Arie and Raine stood still.

It was silent, nothing but their breathing.

The door to the guards' quarters creaked open.

The mean guard pulled the trigger.

Raine fell forward off the stairs, her arms outstretched to Megan.

Arie dropped to his knees with his hands over his ears.

They both heard the pop of the gun.

Megan was as white as a ghost. But she didn't fall. And there was no blood.

Buck dropped Megan and pulled the gun back, a look of confusion furrowing his brow.

In those few seconds, Megan slipped away and Arie leaped forward, smashing his fist into the man's jaw. They both went down. Through the creaking door of the guards' quarters, the no nonsense guard emerged into the hall.

"Granger!" Buck yelled, as he and Arie rolled on the ground.

Granger leapt for Megan. He stomped on the back of her legs as she tried to crawl towards Arie. She yelped.

Raine was at the bottom of the stairs on her knees, and she hurriedly stood. She could run right now. She could run up the stairs and not look back—make it to the roof and down the fire escape. Out of here.

She looked back down the hallway.

Granger was wrangling Megan. Her stomach was to the floor, her cheek smashed into the cement. Her red hair fanned across the ground. He had his foot on her lower back, pinning her down. He struggled with zip ties in his hands, and tightened them around her wrists. The cuffs must have been too far out of reach.

She caught a glimpse of Megan's face. She looked defeated. She wasn't even fighting. She looked away from Raine, to the door that led to the roof. It looked as though she was trying to tell Raine to go. Leave her.

She couldn't. She'd stood at the bottom of the stairs too long.

Granger struggled off of Megan and stood, ready for her. "If you move, I will kill him," he threatened.

Her stomach sank. She heard struggling from behind him. Arie and Buck continued to fight, though she couldn't see what was going on.

"Tell him to stop! Stop!" she yelled at Arie and Buck. Arie lifted his head to look at her, and he took a blow to the cheek. Blood spewed from his lip as he hit the ground. He moaned, and mean guard rolled him over.

Raine slumped against the wall, her hand covering her mouth.

Granger grabbed her arm and yanked it behind her back. She cried out, pulling away for a moment, before he shoved her against the wall.

She stretched her neck back over her shoulder to see Perez's shift partner, who had his arm pressed into the back of her neck to restrain her.

The light from the hallway went out, as did the alarm.

Even though the alarm had been shut off, she could still hear the pattern in her head, her temples pounding in time from the blow.

She was pushed by the guard and marched down the hall, but they didn't turn left into the warehouse. They turned right, straight into the familiar room that still had blood on the floor from what was left of Troy. She kicked her feet. She did not want to go into that room.

"Come. On!" The guard yelled at her through gritted teeth. Behind him, Buck pushed Megan into the room. He went back out and dragged the unconscious Arie by his leg into the room before he shut the door behind them.

Raine had been thrown into the corner. Her knees skidded against the ground as she came to a halt. She turned around and pushed herself against the wall on the floor, her hands cuffed behind her.

She looked over at Megan, who sat with her head down, her eyes wide.

She'd just been shot. Clearly the gun was some kind of prop and not a real gun, but the guard didn't know that. His intention had been to kill her.

Raine could only imagine how frightened she must have been. She herself was terrified just watching it— she couldn't even fathom being at the end of the barrel.

"What the hell is going on, Buck? I leave for two seconds." Granger brushed his hands off on his thighs, out of breath.

"Why isn't Perez working?" she asked, her voice cracked.

"Shut it!" Buck spat in her direction. He wiped blood from his mouth with the back of his hand. He may have gotten the finishing blow on Arie, but Arie tore him up pretty bad first. He looked back at Granger, who was catching his breath, leaning against the door.

"This little bitch was helping them escape."

They both looked at Megan, who looked oddly out of place wearing jeans and a tee shirt.

"Who is this?" Buck asked.

"You don't know who this is?" Granger leaned back on his heels, as if he had no idea either.

"Maybe we kin play with her a lil firs' before we hand 'er over." Buck grinned.

His drawl was enough to make Raine sick as she lifted her head to see him walking over to the delicate girl on the floor, grabbing the front of his pants.

Megan turned her head away. "Not a good idea." Her voice was low, her eyes stared straight up at him, unflinching.

"Oh yeah? You think so?" He asked, grabbing a handful of her shining orange hair.

"He won't like that. Allen doesn't like to share. He'll chop off your penis and make you eat it."

"Who the fu-" He dropped her hair and backed up, his face frightened. He looked over at Granger.

Raine didn't know what to think about what Megan had just said. *Allen must be the Warden,* she thought, half proud of Megan for sticking up for herself around these nasty men, half terrified for her as well.

"Why dun you escort her back where she belongs?"

"That's where I was headed earlier anyway," she interjected.

"Oh *after* you were helpin' these fugitives escape? Where'd you get those keys?"

"Wouldn't you like to know?"

"Take this smart arse back to her Warden," Buck spat at Granger.

"Why don't *you* escort her?" he snarled back.

"He's not going to be happy with you two. You let them escape." She nodded at Raine and Arie.

Raine wished Arie were awake to hear what was going on.

Granger walked over to Megan and reached behind her for her zip ties. "I'm going to cut them. Then we're going to take a walk back to the Warden's quarters. No funny business. Got it?" He spoke quietly to her, though loud enough for Raine to hear.

Megan hesitated before she nodded her head. Her ties were cut, and he pulled her up to standing. "Nobody wants to be in your position anyway," he finished, passing eyes over everyone in the room before he headed for the door.

Megan glanced back at Raine and nodded with her eyes.

I can trust her. She'll come back for us. Raine tried to hold Megan's gaze as long as she could, as if to beg her not to leave her with that mean guard, and the unconscious Arie.

But there was nothing she could do. They left the room. The door shut behind them.

THIRTY

The guard approached her. She looked up at his sly smirk and pale green eyes that made her think of vomit.

"So, what are we gon do with you-tryna escape." It was as though he purposefully slammed his shoes on the ground; as if he knew the sound of his boots on concrete were like nails hammering into her skull.

Arie's presence was completely irrelevant.

Raine followed him with her eyes. "You're delusional."

"S'that right?" He circled around her. "Oh yeah. Yer the psychologist girl. Diagnosing me, are ya?"

"Do you understand that you're not really a guard?" She used her words to try and push him further away. It was her only weapon. It worked with the Warden.

He chuckled and looked down at his chest. He patted his badge and moved his hand to his belt then looked back at her. "Looks like I am."

"Your gun is a theater prop."

"I must a grabbed the wrong one." His eyes narrowed.

She watched his Adam's apple move up and down as he swallowed. She was entirely in tune to body language. And his motions spoke true. He was uncomfortable. He was lying.

"I'd rather be me, than in yer position." He nodded at her. "Sit against the wall."

She didn't move.

He walked up to her, so close she could smell the sweat mixed with pine soap. The same soap she'd showered with in the guards' quarters. He shoved her up against the wall.

Raine winced as she hit the wall. He was much stronger than her, and her hands were cuffed, resting at the small of her back.

Keep him talking, just keep him talking. She peered around him at Arie one more time, then turned her attention back to him. "The other guards don't treat us like this. They don't need to exercise their... authority."

"When I woke up 'ere, I decided there was only one way ta play this game. It's muh choice ta act like this." His diction was syrupy. He wasn't from the Bay area, that was obvious. She wondered how far the Warden, *Allen*, had gone to find victims.

"You were taken from your life too. Like me. You're trapped here." It was worth a try. Maybe he would crack.

"Listen 'ere." He knelt down to the ground in front of her. "We're not out there. We're in here. And in here, I'm the boss." He placed his hand on her thigh.

His touch was like a thousand needles as his crusty hand rested on her bare leg. She recoiled. "See. That's where you're delusional."

He tilted his head in contemplation.

In that second, Raine twisted onto her hip and pulled her free leg up between his. It was enough to do the trick. Her knee landed right between his legs, and he fell over on his side, doubled over in the pain from the blow to his manhood.

While he tried to recover, she twisted and wrestled herself to a stand, all the while dodging him. She pulled her foot back and kicked him in the ribs, and he moaned again. She couldn't think twice about what she was doing, she just had to do it. There wasn't time for conscience. There wasn't time for plotting. Only instinct.

So when Buck opened his mouth to speak once more, she drew her foot back and swung forward, hard, kicking him in the mouth. The kick to the face was painful, sending a lightning bolt of agony up her leg. She must have cut her foot on one of his jagged teeth.

But it wasn't enough to stop him. He grabbed her ankle and yanked it.

She had no time to brace herself, and the impact of her tailbone on the concrete was enough to send shudders through her body. She moaned and rolled away from him. She saw the guard roll onto his back. His face was bloodied, and he still clutched his groin.

She was grateful for her flexibility and small stature, for she was able to pull her arms from behind her back, underneath her butt, and step through them. Even though her balance was better with her hands in front, she gingerly used the wall, as her tailbone and hips were sore from the fall.

"You lil bit-"

Raine pounced on his stomach. She closed her eyes and beat him with her fists locked into a club. As she slammed into him, she thought of every man in her life that this guard represented. Every time she felt out of control. The times she was walking down the street, minding her own business, and had to grip her keys tighter as an innocent man walked towards her. Every time Troy got handsy around her, and thought it was his right to. When she laid her head down on her pillow at night and closed her eyes, only to see the black car at the curb, waiting… lurking…

She squeezed her eyes against the pain cutting into her wrists as she pounded her handcuffed fists down onto him. This person underneath her represented what she feared most in this world. She experienced a sort of release as his flesh ripped at each blow, and the blood sprayed.

She beat him until she heard a moan ring out from behind her.

Arie.

She stood up from Buck, and staggered to Arie, kneeling down by his side.

His eyes were half open, and the pupils large, petrified.

Raine looked over her shoulder at the scene. She froze. "I… I didn't mean… he was-"

Arie reach out and touched her hand. "You had to," he croaked.

The overwhelming sense of regret drowned her. "What do I—What do I do, Arie?"

"Run." His voice was low and scratchy, but plain as day.

"I can't leave you."

"You have to. I can't make it like this. You can make it."

"I'll—" She looked up at the door. "I'll carry you."

"Don't be silly. Go."

She looked down at him, her mouth twitched. "I'll come back for you. I promise." She couldn't stop her tears, salty as they collected at the corner of her lips.

He nodded, his eyes as wide as saucers. "You are so beautiful, Raine," he whispered as he closed his eyes and leaned his head back.

She knelt down and smoothed his hair back. "I promise I'll come back."

He opened his eyes and touched her cheek. He wiped away a trail of a tear.

She closed the gap between them.

He put his lips on hers.

It was soft, and sweet, and it took Raine all the rest of her resolve to back away.

"Go," he whispered, his eyes intense as he stared into hers.

Raine stood up. She turned around and looked at the man she had beaten to a pulp, then at her bloodied wrists. He had the keys to her cuffs. She walked over to him and knelt down. She avoided looking at his face, reached into the pocket of his pants, and pulled out the key ring.

"C'm here." Arie croaked.

His voice startled her as she looked through the keys, and she looked up at him. She went to him.

He winced as he propped himself up on his elbows.

Raine held out the keys to him.

He sifted through a few larger ones on the top of the ring, to a small key that was tucked in between.

She held her wrists out.

Arie put the key into her cuffs, gingerly holding the back of her hand, and twisted it. The mechanism snapped off both wrists and dropped to the floor with a clink.

She twisted her wrists and winced.

"Warden will probably come back, considering—" He nodded to the man behind her. "You need to run. That door is still-"

"Unlocked," she finished. She squeezed his hand. It was hard to stare into his face, black and blue from being beaten. She nodded and turned from him, rushing to the door. She couldn't imagine what she herself looked like.

"I'll come back," she whispered over her shoulder one last time, before she cracked the door open, and looked both ways down the hallway. The coast was clear, and she darted into it.

THIRTY ONE

Raine left the door to the room ajar and peered up and down the hallway. Voices were coming from past the warehouse doors. From behind her, she heard them coming from the stairwell that led to the Warden's loft. She turned from the muffled sound and hurried down the hallway, headed for the door to the roof.

Though she ran as fast as her legs would take her, it was as though they were filled with cement. The door seemed farther and farther away. Like one of those nightmares where function and senses become impaired. Her legs slowed down, her peripheral vision narrowed. Each time her bare foot hit the ground, not only did the impact jolt up through her leg, past her hip and into her back, but her dominant foot, the right side, was covered in blood, much of it hers, and sent a shock of pain with every step.

She had no time to look back. As she passed the guard quarters, she thought of Brandon Perez.

What happened to him? Where is he now?

When she got out of here, she would find his wife and deliver the news that he was still alive. At least the last time she'd seen him, he was. And he'd had a major role in helping her survive. She'd go back and save him.

There was no time to look for him now. The voices were getting louder, closer.

She reached the door, and for a split second before her hand wrapped around the handle, she had a moment of sheer panic. What if it was locked? She should have taken Buck's keys, instead of leaving them behind after Arie relieved her of the cuffs. The brass knob was cool against her skin. She twisted, and pulled the door open.

Unlocked!

The sun greeted her again, blinding her briefly. She started up the cement steps. In her haste, she slipped and slammed her shin into the edge of a stair.

She cried out and crawled up the rest of the stairs with both hands and feet until she reached the top.

The stairwell opened out to an expanse of bare roof. The perimeter was large, with nothing but vast sky and white puffy clouds above her head.

Arie often referred to "the yard" as if he was floating in the sky. They were only brought up here on cloudy, foggy days. And she knew the Warden drugged them beforehand, hence the disorientation and visuals Arie associated with the yard.

She spun around, looking for any signs of a fire escape. Though the walls surrounding the perimeter of the roof were not tall, only about four feet, the top was lined with barbed wire. It looked like a prison yard.

She traced the perimeter of the roof.

She could hear voices down by the door.

If she wanted to escape, she needed to act quickly.

She ran to the fence and put her swollen foot into the chain link, hoisting herself up. Her other foot came next, straight above that. She grabbed onto the chain links directly under the barbed wire and pulled herself up. She couldn't say she'd ever climbed a fence before, but then again, there had been a lot of firsts in this prison.

As she carefully swung her leg over the barbed wire, watching so she didn't catch herself on the barbs, she caught a glimpse of movement in her peripheral vision. She had to focus on the fence before she could look, but as she swung her other leg over and dropped down onto the ledge of the other side of the fence, she heard the distinct voice.

"What are you going to do? Jump?" he asked.

She held onto the fence and shifted her gaze to the hunched over man standing too close to her. His glasses reflected the sunlight, but he was looking right at her.

She didn't answer. She hadn't even looked over the edge yet. *Surely there's a fire escape somewhere?* She turned her body and looked down.

There was no ground beneath the building. Clouds. Fog. She couldn't see anything below. She squeezed her eyes shut and opened them again.

"It's 843 feet to be exact. You're standing on the roof of one of the highest skyscrapers in the city. I own it." The words were sickly proud.

Her body filled with rage. She was losing control. She was out of options. *What do I do, what do I do?* Her mind raced.

"Just walk on the ledge over to the corner and I'll let you back in." He was calm.

That was the last thing she wanted to do.

"Unless you want to die."

The words pounded in her ears.

What would happen if I went back in there? I would die. Die at the hands of a terrible man in a terrible place, or die on my own accord? She couldn't believe she was contemplating the thought, and yet she couldn't seem to find any other outcome for her. Her eyes pricked with tears as she decided her fate, and her body filled with overwhelming anticipation of what was to come.

The man on the other side of the fence stepped towards her.

"Get the hell away from me!" she screamed at the top of her lungs.

He laughed nervously, and looked over his glasses at her. His voice was as cold and deep as the rain on the night of her capture. "Do you think you can escape me, even in death?"

The threat sent a chill through her. Her thoughts raced at a million miles a second. *There is no hope here. No hope of escaping. And I will never surrender to him. That's what he wants.* "You allowed us this little escape so I could find out on my own that there was no way to defy you. You're always watching us. You knew we were going to find out about this roof. We either stay in that prison, or die." Her voice was low.

I would become Meg if I stayed.

"What about all the rest of those people? What about them, Raine? No one will ever know they're here."

She turned away from him and looked down into the clouds again. The words burned in her mind as he spoke them, guilt ripping at her insides. *No one will ever know they're here.* Some of the people trapped in there helped her get this far. Arie, Megan, Perez. She didn't come this far to fail them. And She knew exactly what the Warden was capable of. She'd found that out in the red room with Troy. Troy told her they were in a building just above the city, and that people walked by with shopping bags and coffees in their hands just underneath them. If he was telling the truth, and she jumped, someone would find her and that would lead them to the others. Her head was spinning, but all the pain she felt in her legs, feet, and in her heart had dissipated.

"An unknown fate," she whispered once more to herself.

She looked back at the Warden before she let go of the fence.

And fell.

Fell into the cloudy oblivion.

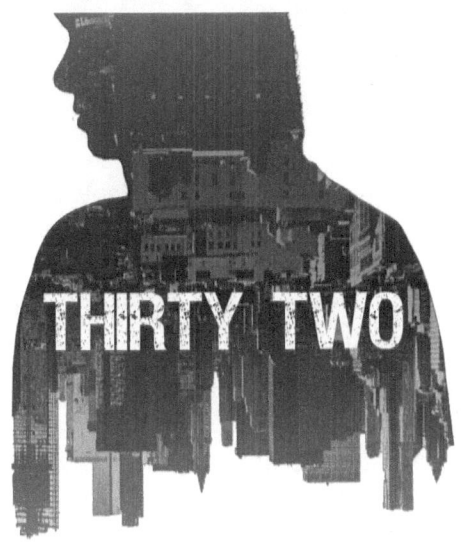

THIRTY TWO

Free fall.

The feeling of complete loss of control. She spread her arms out like a bird falling from the sky. She'd have liked to see where she was headed, but the speed at which she was falling forced tears from her squinting eyes, and she had to close them. The wind picked up her gown and it flapped against her.

In those few seconds, she felt exhilarated and defeated all in the same moment. She'd made the decision to fall. She'd given in to the circumstances. She'd given up. All hope was gone, and she surrendered.

She wanted to allow herself to fall into unconsciousness. It'd be easier that way, but for some reason she couldn't.

Because in those moments, as the wind whipped her hair, she was free.

The ground came quicker than she'd expected. Only she was still breathing. The impact wasn't pavement.

She was alive.

It was a soft, bouncy landing. With her stomach in her throat, she turned to her side, her whole body aching and sore, and gripped onto the unstable surface she'd fallen into.

A net.

Panic set in, gripping her tightly and she looked down through the braided net to the rooftops of the city buildings below. She was still high above the ground, but when she turned and looked up toward the roof, the distance she'd fallen became apparent. The delusional man called the Warden had turned the penthouse of his skyscraper into a makeshift copycat prison from an archived psychological experiment—only he'd glorified the experience and all that came with it for its participants, physically and mentally.

And words she'd heard before she made the decision to fall were flooding back into her now. *Do you really think you could escape me, even in death?*

This was *his* net. It was as though he were a poisonous arachnid, waiting for his prey to send vibration across his web so he could make his way over to them, stick a needle in their vein to paralyze them, and tie their limbs for consumption later. She was his prey, just as she was when strapped to his table.

She'd read an article about these nets once, they were actually called suicide nets. There was talk of a large cell phone company in Asia lining their buildings with these suicide nets because workers were jumping from the high windows to escape the working conditions.

She needed to move. And fast.

She rolled over onto her stomach and tried to push herself up to a crawling position, but the net was wobbly and unstable. She gripped in the braided ropes and pulled her weight over to the side. If she didn't act quickly, Allen would be here to reel her in.

She squinted down to see what was underneath. There was a small alley, of course everything was small from this height, but next to that was another building. From the sky, she hadn't recognized where in the city they were, though she'd suspected they'd never left the Bay area. *Troy was telling the truth!*

If she was caught, she could suffer a similar fate. Though it could be worse for her. She had not escaped just yet. And the guilt of leaving Arie and Megan and the others behind was enough to keep her from wanting to crawl over the edge of the net. But something inside her told her she had to. She'd made this choice, even if out of dire desperation.

She lay with her chest on the net, looking over the edge at the building below. She imagined the flights of stairs the Warden was taking to reach her. He knew exactly at which height he'd built the suicide net, close enough to the building that bystanders down below would never notice it. If they had caught a glimpse, they'd perhaps think it was just scaffolding on the building, something common in the city.

As she looked at the building, she realized what she'd done. She'd jumped. She'd made the decision to kill herself. And that would be on her for the rest of her life.

But right now, she needed to push that aside. This net, a death trap, was also a second chance at life.

She was given a second chance.

Whether it was the wind, or just her imagination, she felt a jolt in the net. A brisk tug. She grabbed onto the braids, rug burn on her palms, and scaled the net all the way until she was hanging over the rooftop of the building below. This was the choice she had.

So she rolled off the net, tucked her arms in, and allowed the fall to embrace her once more.

THIRTY THREE

A sharp pain seared through her arm and up to her shoulder.

This fall was not as cushiony as the last. She'd hit the rooftop and rolled. She lifted her limp, pain-shattered arm and saw a white prick of bone piercing through her skin.

Her eyes rolled into the back of her head as she held her numbed arm against her chest, her gown soaking with more warm, crimson liquid, mixed with the rest from before. She lifted her head and banged it against the roof to try and stay conscious.

"Stay... awake." she whispered to herself. If she faded to black, she didn't know where she would wake up.

And as of now, she was laying sprawled on the rooftop below her captor's line of sight, like a fish flopping out of water. The bird above was her enemy, and could swoop down at any moment to scoop her up. And despite the pain resonating through her whole body, she needed to get out of sight. She inched herself over to the edge of the building. This time she saw a fire escape. She could crawl down the fire escape and get help. Call out for someone to come help her.

This whole time she'd been right above the city. People walked by with their dogs and their briefcases every day. And she, along with many others were right there, being tortured by someone these people probably walked by every day without a second thought.

The thought of climbing down the fire escape brought her deep anxiety over the pain she'd endure. She looked over the edge. A dumpster sat directly underneath, pushed against the brick wall of the building she was on. *If I can make it there, it will break my fall and I can crawl out to get help.*

That was the plan. Jump, or fall rather, into the dumpster below, and then crawl back out and get someone's attention.

She put her legs up over the edge of the building, one at a time. Were feet first a good idea?

She jumped.

But the sight of the bone pricking through the skin on her forearm, overwhelming adrenaline rush from the fall, and the impact itself, were enough to knock her into the black. The green walls of the dumpster and the smell of the rotting garbage engulfed her.

THIRTY FOUR

Her whole world was at the other end of a long tunnel, with muffled voices in the distance. Dimmed lights. A slow, consistent beeping sound next to her ear. *Beep. Beep. Beep.* It throbbed in time with her heart. An unnerving urge pulled at her to follow the sound, and get out of this tunnel.

Oddly enough, as she got closer to the muffled noise, she found it harder to breathe. In fact, her throat was blocked. She reached up to her throat and clutched it tightly, choking. She needed to find help.

The tunnel.

The end of the tunnel.

Raine opened her eyes to lab coats rushing around her and oh so many sounds. One of the white coats pressed her forehead with the palm of his hand and forced a tube up her throat and out of her mouth. It was as though a string with a ping-pong ball attached to the end was pulled out. It burned as it was extracted and she gasped for air.

The lights were bright above her head. She lay in a fresh, crisp hospital gown that tied up the back, on a plank with sheets that were so tight across her legs she felt tied to the bed. She pushed back, shuffled back and forth, and tried to rid the restraints on her legs.

The prison? How did I end up back here? The exhausted energy yearned to move, to break out. She felt like a truck had hit her. Her head was as heavy as bricks, and she could hardly lift her chin to see around the room.

"Shh... calm down, sweetie."

She heard the voice to her left, as others shuffled around her. "I don't... " Her voice was cracked and raspy, as if she hadn't spoken in a while. Her throat was rusty and unused. "Get me out of here." She managed to spit out as she shuffled the best she could. Her arm and shoulder were heavy. It was casted all the way up.

I broke my arm, she thought as she examined the cast the best she could. *How did I... when I jumped?* Slowly, recent events flooded back to her.

Disoriented, she lifted her head the best she could to see where the voice was coming from.

"You been through a lot, so you just relax there, Jane. We gonna find what happened to you one step at a time."

"Where-" she croaked.

"You're at SF General Hospital." A heavyset nurse with red lipstick checked the computer screen. She tweaked a lever on the machine that had a tube running up the side of her bed, into the arm that wasn't casted.

As if she didn't have enough emotion running through her, tears toppled over her eyelids and down her face. She cried, in large salty drops that rolled down her face, into her hair.

She was safe.

The nightmare, for the time being, was over.

Whatever lever the nurse tapped, the pain from every limb, every vein, eased. It was still present, she just didn't care as much. She was groggy, and every ounce of worry and discomfort had dissipated. Whatever was in the clear bag hanging by her bed was strong.

The nurse had called her Jane.

"Jane?" she asked, unable to formulate full sentences both physically and mentally.

"That's right. You're our little Jane Doe."

Raine looked around the hospital room, understanding now the beeping had been a life support monitor, and it tracked her heart rate. She couldn't put everything together just yet, but as her casted arm lay across her lap, she knew she had been saved.

She didn't know how she got here, but she was safe now. "I'm... "

The nurse leaned close to her face, and brushed back the hair stuck to her forehead. "What's your name, sweetie?"

"I'm... I'm Raine Walsh."

"Okay, dear." She looked across the bed at someone on the other side, who was with the sheets and checking different things. "Isn't that... ?"

The voices were too quiet for her to hear.

"We gonna let you rest. You've been through a lot, and we'll get to the bottom of it sooner or later."

Raine heard muffled voices crossing the room away from her. She had a lot to say, but the energy was sucked from her. And even though she was safe, she couldn't help but feel the urgency of what she had to say crawling to the tip of her tongue. Because time was of the essence if she was going to go back and save any of those she left behind-the price she paid for saving herself.

THIRTY FIVE

The sunlight streamed across the hospital room through the window. She blinked her eyes open and closed to get used to it. The sun was warm and comforting on her cheeks. She'd missed it.

The machines by her side continued to beep with the constant beat of her heart, connected to the monitor from the clip on her index finger that triggered her pulse.

Her attention was distracted by the grumble in her stomach. She moved her unbroken hand to her belly and rubbed it gingerly. She'd love to soothe her throat with a vitamin C smoothie. It felt like forever since she'd indulged in her normal diet.

Her attention was caught by voices outside her hospital room.

"What do you mean your waste management doesn't remember what stop they picked her up at? How do you miss that? How the hell did a human woman get all the way to the landfill without anyone noticing?" It was Marcus' voice, plain as day.

She wanted to call out to him, to see him, and achieve any sense of normalcy. But the words they were saying piqued her interest. *Landfill? I was found in a landfill? The last thing I remember was falling into that dumpster.*

"They make multiple stops throughout the city, sir. She could have been anywhere." The second voice was one she did not recognize, one of authority.

Marcus spoke again. "Well why don't you ask *her* where she's been?"

"She doesn't remember much. I think the trauma of her car wreck is impairing her."

"The same car wreck that was more than a week ago? We were told there was a body in the car. Explain that."

"That's classified information. But there is speculation of foul play. We're not entirely sure that the body in the car is the person the car is registered to."

"So you assumed the dead body was Raine's and told her family she was dead? All the while, she's walking around San Francisco? I don't think so."

"What's your relationship with the patient again?"

There was a pregnant pause in the hallway.

"You're just now asking this?" Another pause. "I'm her... I'm her therapist."

"We have no record of her seeing a therapist. You need to leave."

"Fine. I'm her boyfriend. We share an office. We're both licensed psychologists."

"Still doesn't entitle you to any information. You'll have to stay in the waiting room until her family is notified and can get here."

"They live in Ohio. I *am* her family. She's probably scared, broken-"

"Traumatized. She needs rest. You can come back when we've finished questioning her."

"Wait! Marcus!" She leaned forward and yelled out the best she could, though her voice was weak.

"Unbelievable." The frustration in his voice was unmistakable.

She'd give anything to be close to him this very moment. To tell him everything she'd been through.

"Well I'll be back, then. Count on it."

"You're awake!" Her nurse burst into the room, wheeling a tray of food along with her. She rolled up to the bed and adjusted it from laying down to sitting up. "You, super girl, are a fighter." She moved the tray over Raine's lap and lifted the lid. Steaming mashed potatoes and some sort of brown meat covered in gravy were slopped onto the tray. Jiggling red Jell-o in the corner. "You hungry?"

She was starving. But the sight of the food made her nauseated.

"What's wrong, sweetie?" she asked, leaning over and checking the machines. She walked around and lifted a chart down by Raine's feet, and marked things down on it with a pen from her breast pocket.

"It's... okay." She breathed. "I don't generally eat meat. But I'm so hungry."

"Well there's something I didn't know about you." She smiled.

Raine gave her a sideways look.

"When you were out, I had to guess everything. It's wonderful to hear details about what makes you, you.

No longer a Jane Doe. You're Raine Walsh. Risen from the dead."

Raine only partially understood that. There was the conversation with Marcus and the police person in the hallway.

Clips of memories flashed in her mind. Strapped to the table in the Warden's little playroom. The news broadcast of her death in the car wreck. She shivered. "I need to talk to the police," she said quietly, lifting the fork and shoveling some of the potatoes into her mouth.

Eating this food was a big step for her. She was used to her organic, healthy diet. It was something she had control over in her life. Though because of everything that had happened, she just didn't care.

Not only did she escape the prison, but also she felt exhilarated that she had escaped the prison inside her mind—the one that controlled her every move, day in and day out. She didn't have to have so many rules. She just needed to live and enjoy life. And the potatoes tasted delicious. They were warm, and even though they lacked butter and salt, they still weren't the cold mushy oatmeal she'd lived off of the whole time she was locked up.

"Well they'd like to talk to you too," the nurse replied. "But we're gonna monitor it. I don't want your body stressing any more than it has to. So I'll let him in, but the moment you're not feeling up to it, you let me know, baby girl."

"Thank you." She smiled at the nurse. "Thank you for taking care of me."

The nurse smiled and nodded, and walked out of the room.

A moment later, a man in a navy police uniform walked in with his notepad already drawn. The nurse stayed at the door.

The uniform was similar to the guards and the moment she saw it, flashes from the prison flared in her memory. Though his uniform was was navy instead of tan, the duty belt that encircled his hips drew her eyes. She saw the black baton hanging at the back.

She shuddered as she heard the ticking of the baton dragging against the bars in her mind. She squeezed her eyes shut and shook her head.

"Hello." The officer spoke gently. He was young. Younger than she expected from hearing his voice in the hallway.

"When can I see Marcus?" she asked.

The question caught him off guard. "I just have a few questions for you, then we'd love to reunite you with your family. But everyone has been through a lot and we need to straighten out the facts first."

"You don't have to tell me I've been through a lot." Even though it hurt her throat to speak, she spoke swiftly.

He grabbed a small chair on wheels, rolled it next to her bed, sat down on it, and flipped his notepad to the next page.

She looked over at his clean-shaven face. "I heard you in the hall. Why didn't you investigate further into whose body was in my car? My family thought I was dead. Nobody was looking for me... " She trailed off. Somebody *did* look for her. *Troy*. And now he was dead.

"It was an unacceptable mistake in every way. We are truly sorry for that. But what's important is the period of time you were missing. From the time of your car crash, until the time the police were called by the uptown waste management landfill. They reported they found a young naked woman in one of their trucks. We need to fill in that gap. And we're hoping you can help with that."

"When was I found at the landfill?" She tried to get a grasp of how long she'd been at the hospital. Everything was a blur.

"You've been in a coma for about six days."

"What?" She leaned forward in her bed, tugging at the IV in her arm, the bruises triggering a sharp pain in her shoulder. She winced as the machine beeped next to her.

The nurse hurried in. "I knew this was a bad idea, officer. You need to come back-"

"No, please. I need to talk to him. There's no time. You have to catch the Warden. You have to save the others!" She couldn't help blurting out things these people weren't ready for.

She'd been in a coma for a week. The officer's words struck her like a blow. It'd been a week since she'd left the prison. Not hours. Not even days. A week. Anything could have happened within that time.

"Now I gotta redo your IV, sweetie. You can't jump up like that or we can't have visitors." She pulled the IV out of her arm and pressed a piece of gauze to the site.

She didn't feel the pain. She pushed the tray away and turned to the officer. "If it's been a full week since I've been here, then we're too late. We'll never catch him."

"Tell me who he is."

"I only know him as the Warden. He kidnapped me. Locked us up. There were so many of us. Arie, Megan, the tattooed man." She couldn't get her thoughts together and words and sentences spilled out of her mouth like verbal vomit.

"Hold on. How about I ask the questions, and you give me simple answers. We'll figure this out, okay? Your family in Ohio has already been notified. We weren't able to tell them sooner because we didn't know who you were until you woke up, okay? Marcus claims to be your boyfriend? Your colleague?"

"Yeah. I mean… " She wanted to blurt out that they were friends. But she remembered what he said in the hallway. She wanted to see him. Perhaps the argument was stronger if they were together. "He's my boyfriend," she told the police officer.

"We'll get him up here as soon as we're done here, okay?"

She nodded, lifted her hand, and wiped her eyes. As she put her hand back down, the nurse took it. "Hang in there, dear. Your arm has had enough." She looked over at the police officer. "And I've only stuck her twice. There were bruises before she got here."

"How'd you get those bruises, Raine?" he asked, his voice calm.

"We were drugged often. I was unconscious a lot in the prison."

"The prison. Can you tell me where or what this is?"

She took a deep breath as the nurse stuck the needle through her thin skin. The fluids hydrated her veins.

"It was a skyscraper… " She breathed and looked past the guard… *No, not the guard*, the police officer… to the window where the sunlight poured in. "The Warden owned the skyscraper. And he'd turned the penthouse into a prison. That's where he kept us. In tiny cages the size of dog kennels."

The nurse looked as if she'd just seen a ghost. She backed up to the door.

The police officer looked at her before he gripped the pen tighter, balancing the notepad on his knee. "That's a pretty incredible claim, Raine. Are you sure?"

She looked at him. Her eye twitched as she nodded.

He smiled at her and scrawled into his notebook. He continued, "Do you know anything else about this man you're calling the Warden?"

She thought for a moment. "Well I know what he looks like, which some of the other victims can't say."

He scratched something down, and looked up at the nurse. "My partner went down for coffee, can you tell him we need to get a sketch artist down here?"

"No." The nurse shot back.

"Excuse me?"

"I ain't one of your minions. I'm here to see that my patient stays comfortable. I'm not leavin' her. Tell your partner that figuring out her safety is more important than his coffee."

The officer sighed. "Right. Raine, what else do you know about this man?"

Raine looked from the nurse back to the cop. She liked the nurse. She took care of her and had her best interests at heart. She wanted to tell this officer everything, but the more things that came out of her mouth, the more bizarre they sounded, even to her. And if they sounded weird to her, what would the average person think? She sounded like a crazy person. She felt like a crazy person.

"One of the girls called him Allen. That's all," she said quietly. Defeated. "There are others there. He took them, too. He's hurt people. He's raped. He's killed." She leaned forward and grabbed the officer's arm. "You have to find him."

He looked down at her hand. "That's why I'm here." He stood up, allowing her IVed hand to fall back to the bed. "Why don't we take a break here? I need to make a few phone calls-" He looked up at the nurse "-and find my partner. If the hospital allows it, you should let her see her boyfriend." He nodded to Raine. "We'll talk again."

"Joy," she said under her breath, and immediately felt disrespectful but realized he probably didn't hear her. "Officer?"

He turned towards her. "Hm?"

"Brandon Perez. He's from the Bay Area. Can you find his family and tell them he's still alive? At least he was when I last saw him."

The cop hesitated a moment, scribbled in his notepad, and nodded to her. He walked up to the nurse and whispered, "She's not making much sense."

"She's been through a lot. Everything is jumbled in her mind."

"Yeah, but how long until she's coherent?" he asked.

"However long it takes." The nurse put her hand on her hip.

"Right." The officer looked back over to the bed, and then made his exit.

"Thought you said you were starving, sweetie? You barely touched your tray."

Raine looked up at her and nodded. Potatoes didn't sound so great anymore.

THIRTY SIX

"**Y**ou've never looked more beautiful. You know, they said you could still hear things when they talked to you. In the coma." Marcus sat on a plastic chair by her bed, holding her hand. Darkness had begun to fall outside the window, and the lights in the room were dimmed. "I'm sorry I didn't know you were here when they found you."

"I am just so happy to see you. I'm sorry about that night in your apartment. The rainstorm... "

"Shhh. It's okay." He leaned forward and kissed her forehead.

She was comfortable, safe. She didn't have the energy to think about what Marcus was to her. He was normalcy. And though she was learning to build herself up to where she didn't put her safety in others, it was still hard to not associate him with this trust.

"Raine, you've been in a coma for a week. Nobody even knew who you were for them to tell us you were here."

She nodded. "I got away, but so many are still trapped. Every moment that goes by is a moment lost for them. I need to make sure Arie and Megan and Perez and the tattooed man are safe. Marcus, somebody needs to do something about that facility. There are so many people in that prison, and who knows what they're doing to-"

"Hey! Hey, it's okay." He stood and paced from the bed to the door and back.

Her hands trembled as she watched his reaction. *He doesn't believe me.*

"Uh, they said you might do this. You might have hallucinated when you were out-"

"Hallucinated? I know exactly what happened to me! I was drugged and woke up in this prison. Marcus, the cages were the size of dog kennels—you couldn't even stand!"

He took her shaking hand in his. He peered into her eyes, the crease between his eyebrows apparent.

"Don't look at me that way," she whispered, pursing her lips.

"What way?"

"That thing with your eyebrows. You do that thing when you're speaking to clients. I'm not crazy, Marcus!"

"I never said you were crazy. And the clients I help aren't crazy, you know that."

She regretted saying that. It was insensitive. There was a stigma about mental illness that Raine always sought to break. People with mental illnesses weren't crazy. They were dealing with the world in their own way, through their own perspective. She was too. Though she felt crazy. She wasn't sure what had happened to her in the times that she spent unconscious, which felt like quite a bit. She couldn't even recall the date. Quite frankly, the only thing that seemed clear, was the car wreck…

the fight she had at Marcus's apartment, breaking it off with him, the thunderstorm, and then the car wreck.

"I'm going to have to go get a doctor." He started towards the door.

"Marcus!" she exclaimed.

He looked over his shoulder. "You're distressed. They said if any of your vitals spiked—look at that screen."

"I'm just anxious, please stay here. I finally get to be with someone who's not a stranger." Her sentence ended in a whisper.

Marcus stopped and slowly made his way back to the chair on the other side of the bed. "Just take it easy, okay. Don't scare me like that."

"Can you tell me what happened to me?" Raine whispered, looking over at him with desperate eyes. "I heard you talking to that officer. There was," she gulped. "Another body in my car?"

He hesitated, and began the story with a solemn expression. "There was definitely foul play. I was in bed and never got the text that you made it home safely that night like you said you would. I thought maybe you'd just decided not to, you know, give me false hope. I thought you were just telling me we were over for good. But then you didn't show up for work the next day. Or the day after. I went to your house and no answer. Your neighbor let me in because they said they'd heard Viona whimpering all night. You hadn't been back for days."

"Viona!" she whispered with a pained expression.

"Don't worry, I brought her back home with me. She's okay. She's been depressed and mopey, but she's okay."

Raine reached forward and squeezed his forearm in thanks. She owed him.

"But it was then that I knew something had happened to you. You'd never leave your dog. I told police the last time I saw you and what happened. I didn't tell them you broke it off with me." He stifled a small laugh. "Left that part out of the narrative. But they searched the route. Sure enough, your car was in the woods off the side of the road. Still trying to figure out how nobody saw or reported the fire. Except that that storm was so bad. It must have been enough to put the fire out. We didn't know how bad it was until we saw the reports on the news. Your car was totaled, Raine. There was a body burned to a crisp. Unidentifiable. Couldn't even tell if it was a man or woman. Not even dental records would work."

She absorbed that.

None of this made sense. What was happening? The Warden. He had replaced her body with another when he took her. It didn't faze her that that was a possible answer to the equation.

"So then I got onto Troy about it at work. He'd been harassing you, and other women of course, and he'd been acting really weird. I told him we were planning to have that talk with him. We got in a fight, and the next day he was packed up. Said he was leaving the practice. And he was just gone. Of course, that made me suspect him more. And I'm still not quite sure whether or not he had a hand in this."

She tensed up at the sound of his name. She knew how the Troy story ended. He must have packed up when he was getting closer to solving her case. Why would he do that, though?

"My abductor... He was a patient of Troy's at one time. Is there any way to access his files?"

Marcus looked down at the floor, and rubbed his hand over his face. He shook his head. "Gone. All of them. What he didn't take with him, he shredded. I'm still trying to understand the timeline here, Raine. What we don't get is what happened during the window of time between authorities finding your car, to finding you inside that landfill. What happened?"

"I tried to tell you. I tried to tell the others when I woke up. Nobody will listen! I told that officer about the Warden. It was awful, Marcus. Some kind of copy-cat Zimbardo wannabe, said he was going to finish the prison experiment that was cut short. He was referring to the Stanford Prison Experiment in 1971. You remember studying that?"

Marcus nodded. "How many were with you?"

Raine took a moment to catch her breath. She didn't want her heart rate speeding up again as she explained to the only person that would listen to her. "I didn't get a full count, but including the guards... maybe around twenty people."

Marcus reached up and smoothed his chin, slightly parting his lips. "How do that many people go missing and nobody notices?"

"People go missing every day. You believed I died in a car wreck two weeks ago. There was a girl in the prison that had been there two years."

"Jesus," he breathed.

"I just feel like we've wasted too much time. I want to find the guy and save the people I left behind."

"How do we find this, this place?" he asked. "Did you have any indication of where it might be?"

She shook her head and heaved a heavy, rattling sigh. She was kept inside the whole time so she had no idea. She tried to remember what she saw as she lay in the suicide net surrounding the building. *The net itself!* Though he could have already removed it the week she was in a coma. She had so much adrenaline going through her body and mind that she couldn't recall a single detail.

It was equivalent to when something has happened in hurried situations. Like meeting colleagues at a bar for a network event, and realizing after leaving the house that you've forgotten to lock the door, or left your wallet on the table, or forgot to notify everyone of the address. These things that normally wouldn't slip your mind just do, because of the hurry you're in.

Raine identifying the location of the building where she'd been held captive was the same thing.

"All I know is that it's a skyscraper in the city. He'd turned the penthouse into the prison." She leaned back on the pillow.

"You're tired." Marcus reached up and moved some of her hair behind her ear. "You're going to be all right, Raine." He spoke quietly. "The nightmare is over."

In a sense, he was right. She no longer felt like she was bogged down by the anxiety of the unknown. She was more empowered now than she had been since that fall night in her freshman year of college.

He leaned forward and kissed her on the forehead, and stood up. "I'm going to let you rest." He smiled at her and started for the door.

"I know where Troy went," she croaked.

"Excuse me?" Marcus stopped in his tracks and turned his body slightly to look back at her.

"He came after me. And he found me."

"I'm confused. They didn't say anything about Batterman being at the landfill."

"No. He found the prison, Marcus."

A silence loomed between them.

"Is he still there?"

"No. He was murdered."

They had a lot of catching up to do.

THIRTY SEVEN

ust as soon as Marcus left, the nurse came back. She
kicked the door kickstand up and pushed the door
back, humming to herself as she went. Her smock
was printed with purple lilacs, and she had a stethoscope
around her neck.

Raine hardly had any time to herself to think about
what had happened since she woke up, constantly surrounded by people. Maybe what she went through was
all a hallucination from her medication. Maybe Troy just
skipped town. Perhaps she imagined what she wished
would happen to Troy for harassing her and treating
women so terribly. And maybe the whole prison thing
was just what was happening in her head when she got in
the car wreck that night in the rain.

As she contemplated that, she knew that what she'd
experienced was as real as the broken arm that itched
under the cast; the arm that she broke when she jumped
from the suicide net to the building below.

"I just… I just don't understand. I was trapped. It
was real." She looked up at the nurse, who was caught
off guard by her raspy voice.

"You're not trapped inside that coma anymore, Raine, *you are free*." She lifted the bottom of the sheets back to reveal Raine's feet, the right one heavily bandaged.

Trapped inside my own body.

Her experience as a relationship counselor had begun to flood her with theories about herself. Had she dreamed up everything that happened to her when she was inside her coma?

Through her training, she knew it was natural for a victim to feel guilty after an accident, even in their subconscious. Perhaps her subconscious' way of dealing with this situation was to create an alternate reality that she *needed*, to pull herself out of the coma. To pull herself out of the prison of her own mind, that was controlling her life.

And as she thought about it further, the parallels presented themselves: hospital gown. In a prison, would they be given hospital gowns to wear? The bruises on her arm. From an IV drip? And it would certainly explain why there were moments of time where she was unconscious. What were the odds of her ending up in Altruism Prison? The name of the prison that never caught on with the inmates, but that the guard Brandon had told her the other guards called it.

My dissertation was on altruism in the human psyche. Did I just take that and turn it into this big, huge delusion?

The bottom line was that she was safe now. And all that was left was to recover. Reliving stress wasn't the best way to do that. She was going to have to let her story go.

She was going to have to go with the truth.

"Thank you for being here," she told the nurse again.

The woman moved her legs back and forth, bent them at each joint, then rolled her ankle in gentle circles. "We've done these exercises a ton of times, only you weren't awake to witness it. Keepin' your muscles nice and un-atrophied. And you're welcome, sweetie."

Raine allowed her to work through each exercise. "Has anyone talked to my family?" she asked.

"Your mom, dad, and sister are on their way now."

Raine nodded. "Thanks."

When the nurse was finished, she pulled the sheet back up. "Comfortable, honey?" she asked.

Raine nodded again, looking over at the IV bag. What was in there? It must have been strong because her eyelids were growing heavier by the minute, and her head was spinning.

Maybe the jail never happened. Maybe I made it all up... or... Her thoughts slowed down and became more jumbled. A single ray of light from the cracked door bled in from the hallway.

She fell in and out of dreamless sleep, checking the window for external cues as to what time it was every time she woke. Finally when she woke, conscious but not feeling like opening her eyes, she heard voices outside in the hallway. She perked her ears.

"None of her story checks out. We've torn apart every skyscraper in the city! And the one piece of solid information she told the boyfriend, was that the same person that abducted her, murdered Troy Batterman. And that the murderer was one of his mental patients. Only we can't check that out either because Batterman left town few days back and took all of his files with him! If he was going to rescue Walsh, don't you think he'd just have gone and not taken his whole practice with him? Point A to point B just don't add up."

She listened to the detective, wanting to shout out at him that she'd told the truth, only she wasn't quite sure anymore what the truth was.

"So you're telling me the team has already eliminated every skyscraper in the city as evidence that something of the likes of what Walsh explained actually happened?"

"Checked the buildings out from floor to scaffolding."

"There's one detail that just doesn't sit well with me though."

"What's that?"

"The dead body in the car at the crash."

There was a silence in the hallway, a silence that set prickling goose bumps down her limbs. It just reminded her, as if she needed reminding, of the evil this man was capable of. And he needed to be stopped. But if they couldn't even find the skyscraper he held them in, how were they going to be able to catch the man?

THIRTY EIGHT

er eyes shot open. As the light of the moon glowed into her room, she saw him standing near her bed and he'd been more radiant than the last time she saw him. Especially since he was cleaned up. There was a moment of pure panic, as she blinked her eyes multiple times to see if he would disappear, but there he stood in the doorway of her hospital room, as if she'd dreamed him up.

"Arie!" she gasped. Her body tensed up as he took up her hand. "You're not—you're not real," she choked, trying to bring herself to reality. *What's in that IV drip?*

"Huh? What are you talking about? Of course I'm—Raine what are they telling you?"

She looked him over, realizing he was wearing scrubs. He must have been a nurse or doctor of some sorts. He probably assisted with her recovery. She'd made him a character in her little coma story, like the nurse telling Marcus she could hear them while she was out. She was so exhausted at this point she just let him speak.

Arie grabbed the chair and pulled it up to the bed. "Raine, please. I'm sorry if this is overwhelming. I don't know what you've been told, but I know the truth. I was with you. When you jumped, I just—couldn't handle it. In that moment, I felt the weight of my entire life. When you left that room and you didn't come back. I knew you'd jumped off the roof. And I knew the answer. I couldn't let you go. I didn't know if you died or made it."

She couldn't believe what she was hearing. He had just given details from her experience that she hadn't told Marcus. Or the detectives. Or the nurses. She hadn't told anyone. He was in that prison with her. And he was touching her hand. Physically touching her hand. She felt the cool dry skin of his palm on hers. "How did you—" she lost the words.

"After you left, things changed. Megan told me the Warden was packing up. Tearing down parts of the prison. That detail told me that you had lived. He was afraid of outsiders or authorities finding the place after your escape, so he packed up. In the confusion, two of the guards turned on him. They mutinied. They opened all the cages and people were running."

"Brandon," she whispered. She didn't have to ask which guards mutinied. She knew.

"In all the commotion, I was able to find a staircase that took me down. Far down. I ran until my knees buckled underneath me. And I found the sun."

"Why didn't you try to go to the police?" she asked.

"I did. They wouldn't believe me. They thought I was crazy! I didn't know where to find you, I said I'd been with you in the jail, only I didn't know your last name. They said you'd been killed in a car wreck. I thought I was going insane, I thought I'd dreamed you up—that I needed the idea of you in order to escape."

That sounded all too familiar to her. "I thought I dreamed you too," she whispered, astounded.

"And I finally found you. And we can go back and find the Warden and save the others." He leaned forward, resting his forehead on the mattress.

She lifted her hand and brushed it over his ash brown hair. "How is this possible?" she asked.

"I don't have any idea," he replied, lifting his head back up. "All I know is that there are so many people still trapped in that place. Even after the mutiny, I couldn't wait to see if any of the others escaped. So if you'd like to help, I'll understand if you don't—I need to get to the bottom of this."

"By others, you mean Meg."

"She deserves what we achieved." he said, "If she escaped, she'd find me. But… "

"But how will you find him? I heard the detectives out there saying they'd checked every building, he's already fled. The prison is already gone."

A silence loomed between them, almost as though her words were enough to echo through the walls.

"I have to find them," he said. "Raine. Don't share this with anyone else, okay? They're not going to believe you. I've been questioned as well, and I'm not getting anywhere when I try and explain what's going on. We both know what happened. We were there."

"Our perceptions?" she said.

"Huh?"

Raine thought about her training in psychology once more. She remembered the time she'd talked to a patient who was going through post-traumatic stress because of an abusive boyfriend. She was so close to having a breakthrough with the girl about turning the man in, because he couldn't be tried without a confession from the victim. But the girl believed it wasn't the man's fault. She'd convinced herself that the bruises on her body were from falling down the stairs, and clipping her hip on the edge of the kitchen counter.

Perception is reality.

"You're my perception," she told Arie.

"Okay, you're tired. I'm going to let you rest. I'll be back tomorrow, Okay? Hang in there. You're tough. I've seen you in action."

She smiled at him. "Thanks."

"I've gotta go before they notice these scrubs are missing. I needed to blend in to get through those doors. Security is pretty tight down this ward." Arie stood up.

She closed her eyes.

It all made perfect sense. She was content with her reality. "Tomorrow we can start planning that rescue, mmk?" She told him. Her eyes closed, and she heard the door to her hospital room creak before it clicked shut.

THIRTY NINE

Raine lay on her side with her back to the door. It had to be well past midnight. She was exhausted, but couldn't sleep. Staring at the back of her eyelids just brought images of the Warden and the horrors of the prison back to her. When she closed her eyes, she only saw red—red from the fires of her car wreck, red with Troy's blood, and the red of Megan's hair. Red.

She was anxious. She wasn't used to being the one receiving the help. She wanted to get back to helping others. They promised she'd see her family tomorrow, and that was something that kept her hopeful.

The thought of the prison being moved was haunting.

The door slammed behind her and she jumped, heedless of the pain. "No, I'm not sleeping yet," she said to the nurse, who probably came in to check the computers again. The door must have gotten away from her.

"You must be exhausted," the nurse cooed in a sweet, soft tone. It wasn't her nurse in the purple lilac scrubs. But the voice was familiar. It gave Raine comfort and anxiety all the same. She winced as she turned in the bed to face the orange haired, fresh-faced girl.

"Megan. How did you—where's—" She couldn't form any words.

"Shh... Don't hurt yourself now." She walked over to Raine and stroked her hair back on her forehead. Megan was also wearing scrubs. She was clean. It was wrong.

"Arie's in-"

"I've already been to visit him," she smiled, radiating confidence.

This wasn't right. Raine had never seen this confidence in Megan. She was meek and submissive. And Megan was calm. She'd already been to visit Arie but he wasn't with her?

"What's going on?" Raine's voice was shaky.

Megan walked down to the foot of the bed and pulled the chart off. "You've been out for a week." she said, scanning the file. "Didn't think you'd wake up."

"I want my doctor," Raine demanded. Something wasn't right, and the energy from Megan made her uncomfortable.

The orange-haired girl raised her hands in the air. "Ta da! The doctor is in." Her smile disappeared.

"It did take a moment to find you. But after we allowed Arie to escape, we just followed where he led. We knew he'd find you."

Raine froze. *We. What the hell is she talking about? Help!* She tried to scream, but nothing came out.

Megan clanked the chart back down on the end of the bed and rounded the corner to a cabinet attached to the computer monitor. She reached into the drawer and retrieved some latex gloves. She pulled them up on her delicate hands.

Raine tried to move, but her legs were locked in place. She looked over at the IV drip. She could rip it out of her arm and try to run. "How did you get into the hospital?" she asked.

"I work here." She snapped the gloves on her wrists. "How do you think Allen had access to all the anesthetic?" She smirked.

Allen. The Warden.

"You were working together? You were fooling us?" Her voice was raspy, her throat sore.

"Well not at first, of course. I told you I was his first. Two years ago. But then we fell in love."

She's delusional was her first thought. She'd been manipulated by the Warden. And now Megan believed that he loved her, and she loved him. "Why were you so nice to me?" she whispered. She wanted to cry, but there was no time for tears. She needed to keep Megan talking; she needed to come up with a game plan. She was trapped again, in her aching body that was trying to heal. She was just as restricted as if the straps of the Warden were on her, here in this supposedly safe place.

"Well at first I felt *bad* for you. I sympathized. I knew how you felt because I'd been there. But then, when I saw how Allen treated you it reminded me of myself. And... "

"You were jealous?" She half laughed as she asked. "Please tell me you were not jealous. I hate that man! I wanted no part of-"

"Shut up." Megan's voice was cold, and she pulled out the all too familiar syringe from the drawer.

Raine pursed her lips, but was able to utter a muffled "Please don't," as she watched Megan hold up the needle and flick it with her gloved hand.

"What are you going to do to me?" she asked.

Megan smiled. "I'll make sure you don't feel a thing."

The familiar stench of chemicals wafted in. It was the same chemical smell that clung inside her nose when she woke up in the prison. The image in front of her blinked from the hospital room to the white walls of the prison intake room.

If Megan won, right there in this room, right now, then it was over. Raine wasn't about to become a prisoner once more. She was taking back her own life.

As Megan grabbed her arm, Raine yanked her casted arm over, whacking the pale girl in the face. She staggered and Raine yanked the IV from her arm. She kicked off the sheets.

In the midst of Megan's surprise, she dropped the syringe to the floor. This time her fingers curled as she lunged for Raine's throat.

Raine rolled away from her, and braced herself for the hard floor of the hospital. It came quicker than she expected. She landed on her side with a grunt, curling into a ball before she moved. She rolled under the bed, towards Megan's feet. "It doesn't have to be this way!" she yelled. She saw Megan's feet shuffling, as if she was trying to decide her next move.

"You don't understand. I have no choice." Megan kicked at her under the bed.

Raine yanked her chin back to avoid the blow and blindly reached her hands forward, grabbing Megan's foot. She pulled it.

Megan fell on her backside. Her hands flew up to her head.

Raine saw the clock ticking inside her mind. She used her good hand to slide herself out from under the bed, on the floor next to Megan. Megan was turning away from her to push herself up.

The adrenaline was driving Raine at this point, and she jumped up and positioned herself on Megan's belly. She shoved her casted arm up underneath her throat and pushed her chin up.

"Don't kill me," Megan husked. "I saw what you did to—guard— "

That statement partly gave Raine satisfaction, and partly made her feel terrible. Guilty that she was capable of something like that. "Kill you?" she laughed, and caught her breath as her casted arm shook with effort while she pinned the girl she once trusted to the floor. "How will we ever find Allen?" It was the first time she used his real name. She didn't like it. "And if he was really in love with you, he'll come back for you. But I know how narcissists are." She used her other hand to put two fingers on the pressure point of Megan's neck. "And now it's your turn to live in an actual prison." She applied pressure to the point she was taught in one of her many self-defense classes. It was enough pressure to make a two hundred pound man pass out, but not kill them. Megan was by no means two hundred pounds, but Raine felt the weight of the situation underneath her.

As the girl stopped kicking, Raine pushed herself up on her wobbly legs and backed up, all the way to the door. The moonlight through the window shades cast lines on the floor, and lines on the face of the girl who has been imprisoned longer than any of them.

FORTY

Two Months Later

Raine loosened her grip on the loop of the leash as she walked the eager Viona down the sidewalk towards the field of grass. She pushed up the sleeves of her blazer and took a deep breath of fresh air, with her face to the sky as they approached the field. She unhooked Viona's leash and let her run into the dog park. "Good girl, Vee!" she cooed as she stood back, crossing her arms over her chest.

She pulled her phone out of her purse to check on the time, just before she saw the tall, slender, ashen-haired boy walking two mutts towards her.

She smiled the moment she saw him, and he returned the familiar boyish grin. "You look great!" she called out to him, hurrying over to greet him.

The bruises on his face had healed almost back to normal.

She'd just had her own cast removed, although her doctor made her keep the sling and told her to take it easy for another six weeks.

"You do too," he said, and hugged her with his free arm. "Where's Vee?" he asked, looking around.

"She's the one with the tennis ball over there, keeping it from those other two dogs."

"Yup, takes after her dog mom." He smirked.

She playfully tapped his arm, and bent down to pet the straggly, spotted dog by her ankles. "Who're these guys?" She asked.

"I'm fostering them right now, but they both have so much energy, I thought I'd bring them to the Viona play date. Shouldn't you get going?"

She looked at her phone again. "Yeah, I don't want to be late. Thanks for taking Viona, Arie!"

"Anytime, girl. Have you talked to Marcus yet about double dating with me and Poppy?" He bent down and unsnapped the leashes.

"Arie, you know we'd love to. I'm so happy you were able to meet someone that has as much passion for animals as you do." She reached up and touched his arm. "It seems like you guys will make a really great team."

Arie smiled at her, side glancing over to keep an eye on the dogs. "Thank you. I'm happy too." He looked up. "Ah, man. Doody calls!"

She laughed as she looked over to see one of his foster dogs squatting.

He waved over his head back at her, "Have a good appointment!"

"Thanks. I'll give you a call when I'm on my way back." Raine turned and made her way to the train.

She sunk back into the armchair and hugged her notebook to her chest. The smell of the lavender and lilac diffuser relaxed her further. The light purple walls were calming. It was like home. A woman sat across from her on the sofa. "So tell me about your day." Raine smiled at the woman as she opened the notebook. "Would it be okay if I took notes, wrote my thoughts down while we talk? I can put it away if it makes you uncomfortable." She leaned forward and motioned she'd put it on the table between them.

"No, no it's perfectly fine," the woman answered, her voice soft. "My day has been great so far. I met a friend for coffee this morning. The person in front of me, who I didn't see because she left so quickly after she got her coffee, paid for mine. Something that's called paying it forward. Something so small, but makes such a big difference in the life of a stranger, you know? She's not trying to save the world, but the fact that she made my day, and she didn't even know me, it's what humans are made of. I'm sure you can relate. Have you gone to see her at all?"

Raine stopped writing and looked up. She'd told the woman about Megan. "No. My friend Arie has, though. And she's still not talking."

"Have you concluded why the man you called the Warden did what he did?" she asked.

"Well, based on my clinical training, he was your typical psychopath. He believed that what he was doing was for the greater good of humanity, studying human behavior. You know, he could have studied human behavior by just sitting in that coffee shop with you this morning."

They laughed in unison. The woman reached forward and took a sip from her ice water.

Raine continued, "Instead, he took it to the extreme. He was resentful for being excluded back when he was in college."

"A very good lesson for not allowing things that happened so long ago affect your life now, huh?" she said.

Raine leaned back in the chair and smiled. "Yeah, I'd say so."

"What about her—Meg, was it? Was she doing it for the greater good?"

"No." Raine sat back in the chair again and looked across the table at the woman's ringlets, which sat perfectly at her chin line. Though they were in a professional setting, this was a woman she trusted. She felt comfortable sharing these details with her. And if it could help, the sharing was meaningful. "Megan exhibited another example of human behavior. Survival. Resilience. She did what she had to do to survive at first. But then, then she manipulated the manipulator, all in an effort to save herself. Megan's motivations were not for the greater good of humanity. Megan's motivations were fueled by her own sheer will to make it out alive, no matter the cost to others."

"Is that what you feel you did too?"

Raine thought about it. "I've dedicated my life to helping others in spite of my own paranoia and anxiety. I am still a flawed human being, but I would have never killed Megan in my hospital room. And now she's our ticket to finding and rescuing the others."

"It's been two months. You don't think that they're gone?"

"I do." She said with regret. "Gone to a new city. Murdered at the hands of the narcissistic psychopath.

I'm not sure." She remembered what he was capable of. "Nobody can know. I just have to accept that it is not in my control."

"I agree. It's not your fault."

She nodded at the woman. "Well thank you."

"I know you probably feel like you're responsible for the others, but you're not. I'm sure the authorities are working to find them. You've been doing a great job of getting your life back on track."

"Well I appreciate that." She nodded at the woman.

"I'm serious. You've come a long way, Raine, and I'm proud of you. I think you'll be able to get back to doing routine things again soon, maybe get you back in the office with clients again. I'll see you for your next appointment on Thursday, yeah?" The therapist with the curly hair closed her own notebook and put it on the table between them, then inched to the front of the sofa.

"Thursday works," Raine agreed.

"Just make sure you check in with the receptionist on your way out, and she'll get it confirmed for you. Remember, focus on those things that you do have control over. Live your life. Buy a coffee for the person behind you in line, and accept the free one when that person is in front of you."

Raine smiled. "I like that. Thank you, Doctor."

"Any time. Maybe next time you'll be willing to talk about when you woke up in that prison. Tell me the story."

Raine nodded. "Yeah. I think so. Next time."

"Tell me Raine, I'm curious. Why did you decide to become a psychologist? Why did you want to dedicate your life to studying the human mind, human nature?

Was it to protect yourself from what you feared? Was it because you couldn't control your own paranoia and anxiety, so you wanted to see it in others, to see that you were not alone?"

Raine contemplated the question for a moment. "I've always known this answer, from the beginning. It's the same reason you chose to become a therapist." She stood up and crossed to the door, putting her hand on knob.

"I did it for the greater good."

THE END

WANT TO KNOW WHAT HAPPENS NEXT?

Like this story, each book in the series digs up a psychological experiment from within the archives of our history. In book two, Raine Walsh continues her story, but you will also get the perspectives of two other characters: A tireless detective, and a killer that could be your neighbor.

If you liked *The Altruism Effect*,
you will love the 2nd book in the series:

THE
BYSTANDER
EFFECT

Please enjoy this sample first chapter from Book 2 in the Mastermind Murderers series.

ONE

Vinnie

Vinnie shifted in the driver's seat as he watched his prey cross the road under the flooded streetlamp. A young brunette tucked her chin while her jacket whipped around her body in the night wind. The corner of his eye twitched. He leaned forward to the steering wheel and followed her every step. Her long, bare legs.

She's confident. Comfortable. Enough to take her smart phone out and hold it to her face.

When she rounded the corner, he scrambled out of the seat and leaned into the car door to latch it in place with ease. He reached up and greased his hair back behind his larger than average ears. He squeezed his eyes shut, then blinked them open and closed a moment. It was that tick; the one he'd picked up to try and get rid of the irritating twitch that yanked at the outer crease of his eye.

He looked both ways, and crossed the road as he pulled the hood of his black jacket over his head. When he reached the building, he tucked himself around the corner.

She stopped in front of the apartment building entrance and poked at her phone screen. The opportune moment. The fawn stopped to pick a flower, unaware of her surroundings. The perfect target, the perfect prey.

He emerged from behind the corner like a shadow behind her. His brain turned wheels inside his mind. Somehow the handle of the blade found its way from his ankle strap to the palm of his sweaty hand. He lunged, and pierced the knife into the left side of the woman's back.

She shrieked. Her phone tumbled from palm to pavement. It bounced on the screen, and then flipped over to reveal the shattered, blackened face.

It happened in a blurry heap. She tried to spin around, but he yanked the knife back. Another scream. He tensed his grip on the knife and stabbed into her fleshy, lower back. Again. The blade pierced, as if it burrowed into a hunk of pork.

She doubled over and used the door to push herself back upright.

His attention darted to the dangled keys she fumbled in her hands. She must have pulled them from her pocket in the moment she hunched over.

Vinnie spotted the pepper spray on the keychain and he smirked, almost laughing at her effort.

A different voice yelled out amidst the girl's panic, which had almost become background noise to him. It was a man. Vinnie cranked his neck to see the man hanging out of a window from the apartment complex across the street.

"Hey! You!"

He yanked out the blade dripping with dark, syrupy liquid and ran, almost tripping over his own feet.

He rounded the corner and cowered in the alley, holding the knife out so it dripped on the cement in front of him. He didn't like messy. He didn't like blood on his clothing. He regretted his weapon of choice every time. But he continued to go back to the knife. It was as if he'd forgotten all his woes, until after the deed was finished. Plus, a knife was the easiest thing he could get his hands on at home.

A blade required close proximity to the victim. It was quiet, apart from the screaming of course. It brought him a certain release that his mind viciously craved. And the urge ripped him from the inside out. The only way to make it stop was to fulfill the need.

He looked back up to see that the man, who was shouting, had slammed his window shut.

No doubt the man thought it was some sort of bar fight. A common occurrence in the city. Nothing to bat an eye at.

The girl was getting away.

He waited on the side of the building a moment longer for sirens, but nothing came. He peeked his head around and saw the shattered phone surrounded by blood. The girl had no personal lifeline anymore. The door to the apartment stood ajar.

He crept out of the alley with his scrawny back hunched. He crunched the cell phone under his boot and pushed open the door to the building with the sleeve of his forearm. If there was one thing he was good at, it was paying attention to detail. Making no mistakes, making sure every track was untraceable.

She'd made it to the elevator. But no further. Lying in a heap on the ground, her bare legs tangled underneath her. Vinnie kept his hood up as he pursued her. Deep crimson covered her body and the floor leading up to her. He was sure the initial stab wounds were fatal, but it was not enough to meet his urge. He reached forward and flipped her over onto her back to face him.

Her chest rose and fell in rattling breaths. Tears streaked down her cheeks, absorbed her black eyeliner, and set lines down her face. Her eyelids half closed, she stared into his face, biting her lip. "Why—" she croaked, trying to push her hands at his chest.

That was a question he could not answer.

He smelled the liquor on her breath.

It was taking too long to kill her.

His hand forced forward as if his limbs acted alone without the influence of his thoughts. She kicked her legs out at him as he retrieved the knife and stabbed once more. He grabbed her knees and pulled them apart as she scrambled. He heard shouting, blurred words that sounded like a mixture of help and refusal.

"Why are you doing this to me?" she asked between cries and breaths.

"Because I felt like killing a woman tonight." The air was stark. Thin. Cold. The blade was slippery in his hand. He stabbed her one last time in the chest, the stab that jolted her life up through the knife and into him.

Vinnie ruffled her clothing and found her set of keys, pocketing them into his pants. Having the keys would make his job much easier later. He pushed off the ground and stared at the scene, then turned and left the apartment lobby, into the street. He ran to the alley and stripped off his black jacket smothered in blood. He threw it into the dumpster, and took off down the road to his car, the knife still in his hand.

Vinnie closed the door to the garage of his suburban home and proceeded to the corner. He'd built a small shower pan and faucet for washing after coming in from doing yard work. He stripped his clothing, and sprayed all the sweat off his chest and arms. As he held the garden hose with the sprayer at the end, his hands trembled.

What did I do? So much blood. Deep crimson swirled the drain. He cleaned off the knife, and then stepped out of the shower pan.

I had to do it. The urges. The humiliation. He dried himself with a towel and dressed in the boxer briefs he'd left on the workbench. He rolled up the bloodied clothes and stuffed them into a garbage bag, then threw lawn debris over it. He looked back down at himself, his chest rising and falling with hazy breath.

Was that enough? Did I leave a trace? It was sloppy and non-calculated. He'd need to up his game if this were to become something he'd have to do every month.

He turned from his work and headed for the house. The wood floor was cold on the bottom of his bare feet. Tiptoeing across the hall, he avoided every creak in the old house. He reached the bedrooms and turned the knob to a door on the right side of the hall. The moonlight from the window cast a stream of light across the crib as he walked up to it. He reached in and placed his hand on the baby girl's fuzzy head. The energy went through the hand, up his arms and into his chest. The numbing tremble from his fingers and hands had dissipated at the touch of the baby's head. He backed up from the crib and turned, crossing the hall into the opposite bedroom.

He crept around the bed and scanned over the body of the woman inside. She had the quilt pulled over her face.

"How's Scarlett?" she groaned from under the comforter.

"Huh?" he asked, jumping out of his skin at the sound of her voice. *She's not sleeping yet?*

"The baby?" she asked as she turned over and looked dreary eyed at him.

"Oh... yeah... She's great. Sleeping like a baby." He flashed a quick smile before crawling into the cool sheets. His bare chest shivered in the blanket. His wife moaned in recognition to his response and rolled back over.

Vinnie lay there until he heard her breathing catch up to it's usual, consistent pattern. She was back asleep. She'd been loosely conscious the entire time. She didn't realize how long he'd been gone from the room and must have thought he'd only gotten up to check on the baby.

She didn't smell the San Francisco night air on him. She didn't smell the murder.

Follow this link for more:
http://kristinhelling.com/BystanderEffect
Thank you for reading!

ABOUT THE AUTHOR

Kristin Helling enjoys stories with a journey- whether it's a journey across the globe, a journey through space, or a journey of finding one's self.

Kristin studied her Bachelors degree in English writing at Park University, and received an 18-hour minor in Psychology. Her favorite classes were *Positive Psych* and *Social In luence and Persuasion.* It was only a matter of time before this passion found its way into her fiction.

She is married to a photographer, and lives outside of Kansas City, Missouri with their two hairy children: a Husky who is terrified of vacuum cleaners, and a Collie-Shepherd mix with more energy than the sun.

www.ingramcontent.com/pod-product-compliance
Lightning Source LLC
Chambersburg PA
CBHW031340020726
47499CB00005B/1347